"This Christmas only for perfect children?"

"I think the main thing is that they try hard to be good," Miss Lucy said indulgently.

"But suppose be perfect?" Papa demanded.

"Couldn't you settle for being good most of the time?" Emily asked in a small voice.

"All the time," Papa insisted.

Emily glanced at me. "And if we're good all the time?"

"Then," Papa announced, "you can have Christmas."

ALSO BY LAURENCE YEP

The Dragon Prince
The Imp That Ate My Homework
The Magic Paintbrush
The Rainbow People
The Star Fisher
Sweetwater
Tongues of Jade

GOLDEN MOUNTAIN CHRONICLES

The Serpent's Children
Mountain Light
Dragon's Gate
A Newbery Honor Book
The Traitor
Coming soon
Dragonwings
A Newbery Honor Book
The Red Warrior
Coming Soon
Child of the Owl
Sea Glass
Thief of Hearts

CHINATOWN MYSTERIES

The Case of the Goblin Pearls
Chinatown Mystery #1
The Case of the Lion Dance
Chinatown Mystery #2
The Case of the Firecrackers
Chinatown Mystery #3

DRAGON OF THE LOST SEA FANTASIES

Dragon of the Lost Sea
Dragon Steel
Dragon Cauldron
Dragon War

EDITED BY LAURENCE YEP

American Dragons
Twenty-Five Asian American Voices

DREAM SOUL

Laurence Yep

HarperTrophy®
An Imprint of HarperCollins*Publishers*

Dedicated to Uncle Davey

Printed in the United States of America. For information address HarperCollins Children's Books, a division of HarperCollins Publishers, 1350 Avenue of the Americas, New York, NY 10019.

Library of Congress Cataloging-in-Publication Data
Yep, Laurence.
Dream soul / by Laurence Yep.
p. cm.
Summary: In 1927, as Christmas approaches, fifteen-year-old Joan Lee hopes to get her parents' permission to celebrate the holiday, one of the problems belonging to the only Chinese American family in her small West Virginia community.
ISBN 0-06-028389-0 — ISBN 0-06-028390-4 (lib. bdg.)
ISBN 0-06-440788-8 (pbk.)
1. Chinese Americans—Juvenile fiction. [1. Chinese Americans—Fiction. 2. Christmas—Fiction. 3. West Virginia—Fiction.]
I. Title.
PZ7.Y44Dt 2000 99-088636
[Fic]—dc21 CIP
AC

Typography by Carla Weise
❖
First Harper Trophy edition, 2002

Visit us on the World Wide Web!
www.harperchildrens.com

preface 

I grew up on stories not only of China but of West Virginia, where my mother spent most of her childhood. In fact, I have two spiritual homelands—one to the west, across the Pacific, and one to the east, across the Mississippi.

When I won the West Virginia Literary Award, I had a chance to return to my second homeland and explore the area a little more. This is a work of fiction, but many of the events are based on true incidents that happened to my family.

Many of their stories are humorous on the surface, but there is a common thread beneath: that wonderful resiliency of the human spirit—that determination to sink roots into new soil and to flourish.

For flourish they did, acquiring many wonderful friends as well as memories that they passed on to the next generations.

As has been my practice in previous books, I have shown conversations in Chinese in roman type and conversations in English in *italics*.

DREAM SOUL

one

December 1927

In winter West Virginia was white. The newly-fallen snow covered the streets like the icing on long, long cinnamon buns; and it coated the roofs and windowsills like vanilla frosting. The buildings themselves looked as if they were made of dark gingerbread. In fact, it made the whole street look as if it were just out of the oven, and I was almost surprised that it didn't smell freshly baked too.

When I looked at the snowy landscape, I thought to myself that this is the world that a baby sees—all soft and new—with nothing to poke or hurt you.

Snow fills the world with hope again: The rusty rake is painted a shiny white, and the flaking old rooster weathervane is fleshed out plump as a Sunday chicken.

In Ohio, where I was born, the snow had always turned black from the smoke that the locomotive factories threw into the air. But nine months ago we had moved here. Papa thought a laundry in West Virginia would do better than in Ohio. At first we'd had no customers; but the laundry was doing all right now that we had made friends here.

And that had been all right, but I found myself missing even the black Ohio snow. Nothing had fallen all November in West Virginia. Just brown, barren hills and the skeletons of trees and bushes and vines. And it had been cold. But in the first week of December the snow had come—two feet of it. Gazing at all that sugary perfection, I wondered if people as salty and imperfect as us belonged there.

"*Joanie,*" my little eight-year-old sister, Emily, whined, "*hurry up.*" She usually saved her complaining for English rather than Chinese.

I turned away from the window. "*Hold your horses. The snow will still be there,*" I said as I tried to help her get dressed. She kept twitching, though, so it was hard. And of course her stockings were completely wrong.

It was hard to set her to rights, because she kept hopping up and down impatiently, afraid that our ten-year-old brother, Bobby, was having all the fun.

When I had repaired what damage I could, Emily bolted from the room. Her last exhortation of "*Hurry*" echoed down the hallway. I had barely finished dressing myself when Emily came stomping back into the room.

"*Mama says my seams are crooked.*" She held up one leg accusingly.

In winter we had to wear horrid woolen socks that reached all the way up the leg and itched like anything.

"*They're not my seams,*" I corrected her, but I helped

her redo them. Rolling one into a tight coil, I slowly unwrapped it up her leg, smoothing and adjusting as I went so that the seams would be straight.

It was always important that we not embarrass the family, and crooked seams would have had everyone thinking we were sloppy. At fifteen, I was responsible for everything.

When I had straightened them out, we marched back downstairs. Papa had rented an old schoolhouse that he had converted into a laundry. We used the lower floor for work and lived upstairs in some of the old classrooms.

As soon as she heard our steps, Mama called us into the big drying room. Clotheslines crisscrossed the room like intricate lace. Shirts and dresses dangled from them like starved ghosts, and the water dripped from them in a perpetual rain. The moisture in the air condensed on my face, making it feel cool and almost clammy.

Papa sat in a chair next to the big stove, trying to get warm. Even though he had a fire crackling in it, he had tried to ward off the cold with red flannel underwear, shirt, knitted vest, wool coat and pants, overcoat and furred cap. Huddled within his layers of clothing, he looked as wide as a bear. With one mittened hand he lowered from around his mouth the narrow rag that he used as a muffler, and he sipped from a glass of warm milk. Then he quickly covered his face again.

As far as our parents were concerned, there was nothing good about winter. Their misery started with the first drop in the thermometer and did not end until the spring thaw.

I had looked at Miss Lucy's globe once. Our parents had come from a part of China that lies in the tropics, around the same latitude as Mexico. Even so, I didn't think geography was an adequate excuse for hiding indoors all winter.

Mama looked up from her ciphering, which she did with her own system and her own notations. For warmth she had come in here as well while she did the account books. "Let's see," she said in Chinese.

Dutifully Emily and I turned around for inspection.

When she had finished pivoting, Emily clutched Papa's arm. "Can we go outside now, Papa?"

Papa stared at us in puzzlement, as if he could not understand why anyone would venture voluntarily out into snow. "Mmpf," he replied through the ragged cotton.

"Please," Emily coaxed.

Papa relented. "Mmpf," he said.

Mama couldn't let us go without one last lecture. "Now remember. Behave yourselves. You're the children of a scholar. Don't act like savages."

We were always having to live up to Papa's reputation—though even if we had been peasants, it would still be important what everyone thought of us. Between Mama and Papa, I felt like everyone was watching and judging us.

"Yes, Mama," I said quickly. "May we go now?"

Though she still didn't trust us not to disgrace Papa, she grudgingly nodded her head.

"'Bye, Papa," Emily said.

"Mmpf," Papa said. Still puzzled by his American-born children, he raised one mittened hand and waved.

When we got outside, we found Bobby already

involved in a snowball fight with our landlady, Miss Lucy. In her gray wool coat and brown shawl, she looked like a sparrow hopping about in the snow with almost as much energy as Bobby—though she was seven times his age.

"Miss Lucy's got a pretty good arm," Emily said as she watched with a critical eye.

At that moment Bobby and Miss Lucy turned with the same thought and fired at us. I managed to dodge, but Emily caught a snowball in the mouth just as she had been about to make another observation. Spluttering and spitting out snow, Emily began to swear colorful acts of vengeance. The most harmless was a threat to "slit his gizzard."

I frowned in disapproval. "You've been reading some of Janey's trashy pulp novels, haven't you?" I asked her.

However, scooping up a handful of snow, Emily was already charging toward Bobby to begin her revenge. And I followed to help her.

We took turns ganging up on each other until all four of us were thoroughly covered in snow. As we brushed it off and tried to get back our breaths, Miss Lucy panted. *"I do so love this time of year, don't you? First there's the snow, and then there's Christmas."*

I thought of my parents huddling back inside the laundry, thoroughly miserable, and grew quiet. *"We like the snow."*

Miss Lucy wiped some snow from the tip of her nose. *"And you don't like Christmas?"* she teased.

Bobby and Emily just stood there, as embarrassed as I was. We hated to be reminded of the difference between ourselves and our friends. While the town would be celebrating and opening presents, we would be washing the town's clothes—just as we did every other day.

At the same time, I didn't want Miss Lucy to find out how different we really were. I felt honor bound to defend my parents' reputation and not give anyone reason to condemn them for being mean or stingy. "*We like it,*" I said cautiously.

"*What do you like best about Christmas?*" Miss Lucy asked as she shook more snow from her shawl.

From long experience, I had learned how to deflect such questions. "*What do you like about it?*" I asked her back.

That was a puzzler for Miss Lucy. "*Well, I love the music. And giving presents is always fun. And there's always the treats.*"

"*Treats,*" Bobby sighed wistfully.

"*Presents,*" Emily murmured enviously. She'd had her heart set on a porcelain doll that she had seen in the Emporium. And though Bobby said nothing, he was just as eager about the notion of gifts as she.

Miss Lucy smiled as she suddenly realized what her answer was. "*But I think it's the tree. Yes, the tree, when it's all lit up.*" Suddenly a new idea occurred to her. "*Would you like to celebrate Christmas with me this year?*"

"*Oh, Joanie, could we?*" Emily began tugging at my clothes in a shameful display.

"You know we can't," I said in Chinese.

All my life I had wanted Christmas like my friends, but our parents refused. Christmas was not a Chinese holiday, they said.

Sometimes they could seem so mean even about little things, let alone Christmas. There were times in the past when I had wished my parents could be more like my friends' parents.

Florie Adams' parents would subscribe to any magazine she wanted. Henrietta Deems' folks would buy her any sweets she wanted as long as they got their share. Even Havana Garret's father—though he had named her after his favorite type of cigar—indulged her. But not our parents—they never budged on anything.

Bobby snapped his fingers. "Maybe we could. If Miss Lucy asked Mama to a Christmas celebration, she'd have to go along with it."

It would be harder for Mama to refuse her friend and mentor than her children.

For the first time in many winters, I began to hope, and I hugged my brother before he could protest. "Bobby, you're a genius." And to Miss Lucy I said, *"You'd have to ask our parents."*

"*Certainly*," Miss Lucy said brightly. *"The next time I see them."*

"We should get them together now, Joan, while everything looks so nice and Christmasy." Emily was tugging at my sleeve again.

"Bobby should do it," I said, trying to pull free. "He's Mama's favorite."

When Bobby shrugged, miniature avalanches of snow cascaded from his shoulders. "If I really were her favorite, we'd have *Christmas* every day of the week."

So it was up to me, as usual. "We should bring them outside to Miss Lucy, so we can have the right mood."

"That's what I said," Emily stated proudly.

Suddenly I had an idea. "Bobby, you and Miss Lucy start making a snowman," I said.

"Why?"

I was sick of having him always question me. "Do you want Christmas or not?" I snapped.

"Okay, okay," he said, and turned to Miss Lucy. *"Can we make a snowman?"*

"Try and stop me," she said.

"Come on," I said, taking Emily's hand, and we turned back toward the laundry.

I was tired of feeling like a foreigner. This year we were going to have Christmas same as everyone else.

two

However, it wasn't easy trying to coax our parents outside. Papa refused to budge from his chair.

"Papa," I wheedled, "why don't you come outside? It's beautiful."

Emily added her two cents. "The snow's all soft and deep and white. Like the whole town's sinking into a sea of cream." She smacked her lips. "Just looking at it ought to make you hungry."

"Mmpf," he replied through his rag.

Mama put her pencil down. "Your papa will go outside when it's warmer, in the spring."

"But it's only December," I protested.

"Mmpf!" Papa insisted.

"When it's spring," Mama interpreted.

"Help us make a snowman, Papa," I urged him.

Emily was quick to pick up on my cue. "Please, Papa, please." She pulled at his sleeve. "You said you were going to help me make a snowman. Come on, before it melts."

Papa muttered something that Mama interpreted as "When?"

"A long time ago," Emily said.

It was hard for Papa to turn down an eight-year-old, but he tried. "Mmpf," he said, shrugging.

"Leave your father alone," Mama snapped. "He's not used to this cold."

I caught hold of his other arm and tugged. "You've been here eighteen years. You must have gotten used to it by now."

"Mmpf!"

Mother slammed her ledger shut. "Never. At home in China the sun gets into your bones and never leaves."

America was home and not China, but I didn't say that because it would start another argument.

"Please, Papa." I decided to play my trump card and bent over close to whisper in his ear. "I know Mama wants to go outside, but she won't unless you go too."

Between his furred cap and rag, Papa's eyes turned as he glanced at Mama. "Mmpf?" he asked.

Squinting one eye, Mama began to thread a needle. "Aren't you the contrariest man? I thought you didn't want to go out."

Papa gazed at her intently. "Mmpf. Mmpf?"

"Well," Mama allowed, "I wouldn't mind getting some fresh air." Business had picked up so much that we rarely had time to play even on a Sunday like today.

Putting his hands on the arms of his chair, Papa shoved himself to his feet. In the motion of rising, his rag had loosened its coils around his mouth. "Then let's go."

Mama pointed at the glass of warm milk on the table. "Finish your warm milk first." Miss Lucy had convinced Mama that we should all drink more milk. "Your bones have to be strong if you're going to play with the children."

Papa dutifully sipped his milk. "Ugh—it tastes so greasy. I just hope it warms my bones up as well."

Since Mama was wearing only a sweater, she insisted on armoring herself against the cold in coat and gloves. In the meantime Papa rewound his old rag around his head.

When we stepped outside, Mama held on to me for dear life. She was deathly afraid of slipping and breaking a leg. "Mind the ice," she said, squinting anxiously at the snow for hidden patches.

Papa was even worse, though. As Emily escorted him, he took slow, timid steps, as if any moment he were going to sink through the snow and disappear into all that whiteness. Papa was often a fish out of water here in America; but during the winter he really stuck out as different, even odd. As he shuffled, I felt almost sorry for him and ashamed for trying to manipulate him.

Miss Lucy and Bobby were already rolling the snow into a large ball.

"Hello, neighbors," she called when she saw us.

"How do you do?" Mama returned politely in English. She had been taking private lessons from Miss Lucy.

Emily tugged at me. *"Let's make a snowwoman."*

Bobby stopped shoving at the snow for a moment. *"You can't do that."*

"Show me where it says it in the rules," Emily shot back.

"Don't fight in public," Mother reminded. "You're the children of scholars."

I spoke up quickly, before the other two could argue and get us deeper into trouble, destroying any chance of Christmas. I turned to Papa because it was his reputation Mama had invoked. "We're sorry, Papa." It seemed as if I was always apologizing even when I didn't feel the least bit sorry.

Papa's eyes had crossed as he regarded a stray snowflake on his nose. It seemed like the final indignity. "Mmpf," he said, and slapped his arms as he shivered miserably.

"Your father says it's all right," Mama said.

"Race you!" Bobby called to Emily.

Emily was still young enough to accept that challenge automatically—even when she didn't have much hope of winning. *"Come on, Joanie."*

"Help us, Mama," I said, more out of form than out of faith. Up to now, as the wife of a scholar, Mama had always thought she had to be as somber as an undertaker out in public.

However, the sight of Miss Lucy playing must have changed Mama's mind. She glanced at Papa, who gave a barely perceptible nod of his head.

While Emily and Mama set to rolling one snowball, I started on another. Even Miss Lucy got caught up in the race. She was hurrying so much that she lost her balance entirely and fell on top of her and Bobby's half-finished snowman.

By now Emily's snowball had grown to the size of a small boulder. "We win!" Emily shrieked, and patted the snowy sides.

Bobby, though, could not stand to lose. He gave her a push, so she fell into the snow boulder. "Now you have to start o—" He never got to finish because Emily flung a handful of snow right into his mouth.

I was starting to laugh when a pile of snow landed on my head. I turned to see Mama grinning. For once Mama managed to forget her dignity. When she smiled, she looked more like my older sister than my mother.

Then a snowball hit my back. I twisted around. It was Miss Lucy's turn to smile. Something made me duck in time, and the snow Mama flung missed me but got Miss Lucy.

Then I lost track of who did what to whom. All I knew was that you flung snow at anything that moved. Papa remained still as a statue in the middle of the battlefield, afraid to move for fear of losing his balance.

"Excuse me," a man said.

All of us stopped. Until now we had been ignoring the noise in the street, so we had not noticed the sleek automobile that had stopped at the curb. It was cream colored, with huge chrome-covered pipes and an engine that purred like a giant cat as it idled by the sidewalk.

Behind the wheel sat a man with wavy blond hair and a thin, natty little mustache to match. With his chiseled chin, he looked as if he had stepped straight out of an advertisement for Arrow shirts.

Next to him was a girl about my age. She had a long, elegant neck that reminded me of a swan, and a peaches-

and-cream complexion like every heroine has in the magazine stories. She was wearing a cloche, a close-fitting hat shaped like a thimble. Curling across her forehead from beneath the brim was a strand of coppery hair. Her coat had a white fur collar over wine-red velveteen cloth that matched her hat. And her hands were hidden in a muff made from the same fur as her collar.

The girl was pretty enough to have been a model too. In fact, looking at them, I thought I was looking at an advertisement in one of Florie Adams' glossy fashion magazines. The pair seemed to belong to a different world from mine.

The man raised his hat. *"Has the house been rented yet?"* The way he asked, it sounded as if his heart would break if it had been.

In back of the laundry next to Miss Lucy's was a small cottage. She had been using it for storage until recently, but I think she needed the money.

Miss Lucy brushed the front of her dress self-consciously. Her hair had become undone, and there was snow in it and all over her clothes. All of us looked a sight.

She did her best to tidy herself as she took in their fine automobile and clothes. *"The cottage only has one bedroom. Are you sure that will be suitable?"*

"My daughter and I love adventure. In Paris we stayed in a lovely little pension on the Left Bank rather than in some remote tourist hotel. We really got to experience the city that way. And it beat a muddy trench any day." His smile revealed teeth that were as white and even as an advertisement for tooth powder.

Bobby stared at him excitedly. "*You were in the Great War?*"

The man set his hat back down, tilting it at a rakish angle upon his head. "*The War to end all wars, or so they said—though from the state of the world, that seems doubtful.*"

Miss Lucy high-stepped through the snow toward them, leaning her head first to the left and then to the right to study them from different angles. "*That's Quincy Barrington's profile if I ever saw it.*"

Astounded, Mr. Barrington slapped the steering wheel with both hands. "*How astute. He was my grandfather. Did you know him?*"

"*Yes, and I taught your father before they moved to Pittsburgh.*" Miss Lucy brushed herself off. "*Back when I was still teaching school.*"

Mr. Barrington blinked his long, curly lashes. "*Not* THE *Miss Bradshaw? You taught my father the three R's.*"

Miss Lucy folded her arms and pursed her lips. "*So you're Josiah Barrington's little boy.*"

"*Guilty. I'm James. And this is my daughter, Victoria. We've just returned from abroad. But you can't be Miss Bradshaw anymore.*"

"*Still quite the miss,*" Miss Lucy said.

"*The men in this town are fools,*" Mr. Barrington said. Then he gave an amused glance at the laundry sign that Papa had hung up over the front last spring. "*I wasn't aware my father had attended a laundry.*"

"*When I closed the school, it was turned into a laundry by the Lees.*" Miss Lucy indicated Mama, who was still trying to straighten up.

"Indeed." Mr. Barrington seemed to notice us for the first time.

"How do you do?" Mama said politely.

"I suspect we'll be in the same school," I said to the girl.

There was an awkward silence while the couple continued to study us from the safety of their car. Their foreheads were furrowed as if in puzzlement. They stared hardest at Papa, as if they found Papa's clothes distinctly odd.

I had seen that expression often enough—like someone who had found a photo with the wrong caption. We were nothing like the Chinese in the stories or the satirical cartoons: We dressed like American children and spoke English.

Sometimes people then tried to make the round peg fit into the square hole. They would mock us and make strange singsong noises, trying to imitate Chinese. And I found myself tensing.

Victoria was the first to recover. She had the same dazzling smile as her father. She extended a hand, and I saw it was covered in the most expensive-looking glove I had ever seen. It was of black kid leather with a pearl clasp, and there was a cuff at the wrist that ended in a scalloped edge like a bat's wings. Geometric designs had been embroidered on the back.

"I suppose we will," Victoria said. *"And your name?"*

Though we had only met, I found myself wishing I could be as elegant as her. I wanted it so badly that I ached inside. I gave her credit for treating us like any other American children. *"Joan. Joan Lee,"* I said, and I introduced my family.

"Charmed," Mr. Barrington said, and sounded as if he meant it. *"But we didn't mean to interrupt you."*

"It was nothing." Miss Lucy waved a hand in the direction of the alley leading to the cottage. *"Would you like to see it?"*

"But I think someone was assaulting your honor, Madame," Mr. Barrington said. Opening the door, he got out of his car. Heedless of his elegant, tailored clothes, he knelt and scooped up some snow. Before any of us could react, he threw a perfectly shaped snowball at Bobby.

With a laugh Victoria hopped out of the car and, her costly gloves still covering her hands, flung handfuls of snow on her father. The next moment we were all whirling around like dervishes, madly throwing snow at the nearest target.

Only Papa remained frozen as stiff as a snowman. I couldn't help comparing Mr. Barrington with Papa, who was huddling so miserably there. The thought of him made me feel guilty suddenly. He had made his own sacrifices for us, leaving China to come here.

"Mmpf!" Papa finally shouted. Though I couldn't understand his words, his tone was clear. He didn't think a scholar's family should be roughhousing.

Afraid that we were losing Christmas before we had even had a chance to ask about it, I grabbed Bobby. "Stop. Papa's getting mad," I said. Mama stopped of her own accord.

Mr. Barrington retrieved his hat, brushing the snow

off the brim. *"I suppose we'd better look at the house."*

Miss Lucy patted her hair back into place. *"This way,"* she panted.

Over his old rag, I saw Papa's eyebrows draw together into an angry black vee. "Mmpf!" Papa said angrily to Mama.

"I'm sorry," Mama said, hastily straightening her clothes.

Papa turned to us. "Mmpf, mmpf, mmpf!"

"We're sorry, Papa," I apologized.

The Barringtons returned with Miss Lucy. They could only have peeked inside her cottage, but then there wasn't much to see in it. *"I'll dust it out,"* Miss Lucy was saying. *"You could move in tomorrow."*

"Splendid," Mr. Barrington said with his usual cheerful vigor. *"It will be nice to leave the hotel."*

As he and his daughter passed us, Victoria waved. *"We'll see you presently."*

As we watched the car chug away slowly, Miss Lucy planted a fist on her hip. *"He never even asked about the rent."*

Bobby had run to the fence. *"With his kind of money, he doesn't have to worry. Did you see that car?"*

"When Quincy was his age, every girl in town had a crush on him. They used to trail him around like a herd of moonstruck calves." Miss Lucy waved her hand in the general direction the Barringtons had taken. *"I'd heard that the son, Josiah, had gotten into oil and really struck it big. So I guess prices are the last thing on the mind of Quincy's grandson."*

Mama always tried to turn an experience into a lesson. "And he wouldn't be the first son to waste the father's money. For a man who drives such a fancy car, why does he wear a shirt cuff that's frayed?"

"I didn't see anything like that," I said.

"You were too busy looking at the car and the fancy manners." Mama sniffed.

Mama was always finding fault with people, including strangers—even if the faults weren't there. I just thought Mama was being jealous.

Emily looked over the fence wistfully. *"I'd settle for a flivver if I could just have a ride in it. I've never gotten to ride in any car."*

Mama pulled her away. "Cars are for lazy people."

"Uncle Bing has one," Emily countered. He was Papa's oldest brother, who lived in the Pittsburgh Chinatown. Though we had been promised a ride in his car, so far we hadn't been able to get up there to collect.

"Your uncle Bing never grew up. He always has to have the latest toys, and then his little brothers have to help him pay for them." Mama pulled Emily from the fence. "Come on. Let's finish our snowman."

"Snowwoman," Emily corrected her. "And it's going to be better than Bobby's."

As Emily and I labored side by side, she whispered to me, "Tell Mama and Papa about Miss Lucy's invitation."

"Not yet," I answered in a low voice. I felt that the snowball fight had rubbed Papa the wrong way.

"When are you going to ask her?" Bobby asked out of the corner of his mouth. "On Christmas day?"

"Please ask her," Emily begged. "She's never played in the snow before. So maybe she's changed her mind about that too."

Bobby was heaving one globe of snow on top of another at Miss Lucy's direction.

"You're both scaredy-cats," I informed them. As the only one with courage, I turned around—even though I already suspected what the answer would be. *"Miss Lucy,"* I reminded her, *"didn't you have something you wanted to ask our parents?"*

She slapped a hand to her forehead. *"Between snow fights and new tenants, I forgot."* And then she turned to Mama. *"Would you like to celebrate Christmas with me this year?"* she asked.

It was hard for Mama to turn down her special friend. *"You too kind, but no."*

Miss Lucy tried hard to hide her disappointment, but it still showed. *"I can understand your wanting to celebrate in private."*

"Now you've hurt her feelings, Mama," Bobby said.

"We not celebrate," Mama tried to explain hurriedly.

Miss Lucy was puzzled now. *"Well, yes, I know you're not Christian. I was referring to the tree and treats."*

"We not do that," Mama tried to explain. Her mouth worked as she struggled to find the right words in English and wound up falling back on repetition whenever she became desperate. *"Spoil, spoil children."*

Miss Lucy's forehead wrinkled as she tried to comprehend Mama's reasoning. *"But it's a special time of year for the little ones."* She added, *"My celebration wouldn't be anything elaborate."*

Mama hated to disappoint her friend. She turned slowly in the snow and looked at her frozen husband. "Papa, what do you say?"

Papa knew enough English to follow what was happening. He took a deep breath and pulled down the rag covering his mouth. "This woman interferes too much. She might badger us into drinking milk, but she can't tell us what to think." Hastily, he pulled the rag back up before his lips froze.

"My husband say no," Mama said. She looked relieved that Papa was going to play the villain.

Miss Lucy got her schoolteacher look, the one she had when she had lectured my parents on the virtues of milk. *"Mr. Lee, the holiday is about sharing and giving. Surely you can't argue with those sentiments?"*

Papa's eyebrows drew together again in another stormy vee, and he pulled down the rag again. "She's at it again. Why can't she leave us alone?"

However, before he could snap at Miss Lucy, Mama raised her hands. *"We just can not."*

"Mama, what harm would it do?" I asked in Chinese. "It's hard to watch everyone else celebrating. It makes us feel left out."

Mama stared at me in silent reproach, as if I should know better because I was older. I was sure she was going to scold me about this sometime. "We still have to pay for the laundry equipment and our moving expenses. You know we can't afford presents."

As befitted someone who had gotten good marks in public speaking, I marshaled my arguments. I figured that first we had to get our parents to agree to Christmas in principle. Then we could work on the idea of giving presents. "We don't need presents. Just let us look at Miss Lucy's tree and maybe share some treats. Please, Mama, let us do that much. Everybody else does it. You don't want the neighbors to think we're funny."

"And I suppose if westerners brought a pig into the house, you would want one too," Mama said stubbornly.

"You children are becoming too American," Papa sighed. "What are you going to do when we get rich enough to go back to China?"

There wasn't any place in the new Chinese Republic for scholars who could quote from the ancient classics. Everyone there wanted to build factories and make money. So to earn a living, Mama and Papa had gone to Ohio, where they had run a laundry. And seeing a better location, they had shifted to West Virginia. But their dream was always to return to China, where they were born.

However, we had been born in America. China was just stories. Bobby and I knew enough to keep our mouths shut, but Emily muttered, "Not that again."

I hunched over and whispered to her, "You don't want to nip Christmas in the bud, do you?"

Mama had heard her, though. "That's another reason we don't have Christmas. You're Chinese. You should be celebrating Chinese holidays, not American ones."

If Emily had kept her mouth shut, I could have worked on our parents and maybe worn them down gradually, but Emily was too impatient for that. She had to go on wheedling. "Please, Papa. Please, please, please. We'd be the best children ever if we could have

Christmas. We'd do everything you said, and you'd never have to scold us."

Papa got this real sly look. I almost thought I could see his cheeks broaden, stretching his rag as he smiled. Pulling the rag down, he asked Miss Lucy, *"This Christmas only for perfect children?"*

"I think the main thing is that they try hard to be good," Miss Lucy said indulgently.

"But suppose be perfect?" Papa demanded.

"Couldn't you settle for being good most of the time?" Emily asked in a small voice.

"All the time," Papa insisted.

Emily glanced at me. "And if we're good all the time?"

"Then," Papa announced, "you can have Christmas."

"Oh," Emily tried her best to hide her disappointment. "And if not?"

Papa shrugged. "You can't."

Miss Lucy had been anxiously hovering nearby. *"Will you be able to celebrate Christmas with me?"*

This way he could spare Miss Lucy's feelings and not compromise his principles. *"Children good, they can. Children bad, they not,"* Papa said.

Miss Lucy seemed taken aback. *"That seems a little harsh, doesn't it?"* she asked.

For a moment I was afraid that Papa was going to tell her not to interfere. However, he simply turned. *"Christmas only for special children."* With Mama he went back inside.

"You and your big mouth," Bobby said to Emily accusingly.

"Shut up, Bobby," I snapped. Emily looked ready to cry.

That was the trouble with being the oldest. I was always the one who had to console the others. There was never anyone to console me.

"I don't think I can do it, Joanie," Emily said, shaking her head miserably.

"Sure you can," I whispered. "You like plays and you like music. Think of this as a big game of pretend. You only have to act like a good girl."

For a moment I thought Emily would burst while she hunted for the right word. Miss Lucy had been trying to expand her vocabulary, but mostly Emily remembered the less edifying words. Finally she settled on an apt expression. *"Twaddle."*

three

Late that afternoon, as we slogged through our back door into the kitchen, Emily grumbled, "*Why do we have to be good if we're not getting presents? What's the point of Christmas?*"

"*You haven't been around as long as I have,*" I explained. "*It's a lot for them just to let us celebrate with Miss Lucy.*"

Bobby nudged her. "*You can't expect Mama and Papa to give in on everything on the same day.*"

"*Oh,*" Emily said thoughtfully, and her voice grew hushed and wondering. "*I know what I want. I saw it in my Monkey Ward catalogue. It's a doll. She has long golden curls and eyes that really close when she goes to sleep.*"

As far as I knew, we didn't own a Montgomery Ward catalogue. "*Where did you get a catalogue from?*"

"*From Janey's.*" She began to jab the buttons out of

the coat buttonholes. "Want to take a peek?"

I knew my little sister and how bullheaded she could be. *"You didn't just take it, did you? You asked Janey for permission?"*

Emily shrugged. *"Sure, but they had lots. Different years."* She pantomimed hanging something up. *"There was a whole row of them hanging on hooks in her grandpa's outhouse. The one I have is from last year, but it's the same as the new one in the house. Isn't it nice of them to have stuff to read there?"*

"Oh, no," Bobby groaned as he dragged his hat off his head. He was getting the same suspicions I was.

I slipped out of my coat. *"That's not the reason the catalogues are there."*

Emily let me help her out of hers. *"Well, then, why—?"*

Bobby slapped his hat against his leg. *"They're there as toilet paper, you dope."*

"Oh," Emily said in a small voice. She clapped a horrified hand to her mouth. *"No wonder Janey looked sorry for me when I asked for the old catalogue."*

I covered my face in chagrin. *"What must her family think of us? They'll think we don't even have a catalogue to use as toilet paper."*

"Whatever you do, don't tell Mama," Bobby warned as he hung his coat up.

"I wouldn't dare," Emily said. If I was the worrywart in the family, she was the pragmatist. *"Did you want to see the catalogue, Bobby?"*

Bobby jammed his hat on top of the coat as it hung from the peg. *"I already know what I'd like. I want a sled, a Flexible Flyer. That way I wouldn't have to borrow one all the time."*

"Dibs. I get to ride it on Christmas," Emily said.

I knew better than she did what our finances were like. While we were comfortable, there was not much money for extras, and Christmas, I'm afraid, was an extra. *"Even if we get presents, they might not be big ones."*

"And we have to be perfect. Nobody's perfect." Bobby sighed. *"Especially you, Emily."* And he gave her a nudge.

Emily shoved him back. *"You're the one who's always getting in trouble."*

Mama's voice drifted down the hallway. "Are you fighting already?"

Bobby silently mouthed, "You see?"

I took both of them by the shoulders. "No, Mama," I called. "We were just going to wash up for supper."

"That's good," Mama said. "I would hate to end the Christmas contest so soon."

"Before we can even think of presents, we have to be good for the next two weeks," I whispered to them. *"This is like an endurance test. It has to be a team effort."*

Bobby eyed Emily. *"I'll promise if you promise."*

Emily spit on her fingers and held them out. *"I promise,"* she said, and glanced at me expectantly. *"We're going to win the Christmas contest."*

Even though I felt terribly silly, I did the same and pressed my fingers against hers. *"Promise."*

Bobby copied us and held his fingers against ours. *"Okay."*

As we went to clean up, Emily poked me. *"Do you know what you want, Joanie?"*

I did. On the windowsill of Miss Lucy's kitchen was a glass fairy light. The fairy light came in two pieces. The bottom half was a base, from which rose a stem that swelled out into a candleholder. The top half was about the size and shape of a pinecone with a hole on top to let out the smoke.

A deep cranberry, in the daytime the fairy light burned like a coal, like a flower on fire, like a fragment of sunrise. It was an especially cheery, warm sight on a dark wintry afternoon.

However, even if we won the contest, I knew my parents could never afford such a thing.

"Peace and quiet," I said.

"Fat chance of that with Emily around," Bobby said.

Emily balled a hand into a fist and started for Bobby before I caught her by her dress collar. *"Remember your promise,"* I reminded her.

Emily flexed her fingers. *"Okay, but just wait until the day after Christmas."*

Supper was simple that Sunday. Mama had made rice with salted Chinese vegetables that relatives had shipped from China. Cutting it up Chinese style, Mama could make a half pound of ham satisfy five people.

Papa had loosened his muffler so he could eat. "It's snowing again," he said gloomily as he gazed out the kitchen window. Snowflakes whirled by outside as if the air were filled with coarse, white ash. "No green, no color, no warmth. Just this ugly cold white."

Except for winter, Papa was the sunniest man and

always liked to laugh. However, the snow and the cold made him gloomy as a storm cloud.

I tried to cheer him up. "Snow can be fun sometimes. Didn't you like making the snowman, Papa?"

He sighed. "Snow always makes me want to be back in China."

Bobby and I shot warning looks at Emily not to protest that we didn't want to go there. However, for once Emily thought first with her brain rather than her mouth. She made a point of pressing her lips together and drawing her fingers across them as if she were closing up a zipper.

As we began to dine, I thought I should talk about something safe, like books. I couldn't always tell when Mama or Papa might misinterpret our actions or words. And they wouldn't be in too good a mood now that it was snowing again.

As I spooned vegetables onto my plate, I said to Emily, "*You really should read a book that Miss Lucy lent me. It's all these wonderful stories from Wales.*"

"*Wales?*" Papa asked. "I thought those were big fish."

We often acted as reference books for our parents. "It's a country near England," I said.

He shook his head sadly. "I think you hear too many foreign stories." I couldn't understand why Papa looked so disappointed.

Emily, though, got to the important question. "Do they end happily?" she demanded.

"Some of them," I said.

"Then I don't want to read them." Emily wrinkled

her nose, making it obvious why she didn't rate the stories higher.

"But you'll love them," I said. "They're all full of magic."

"There's no such thing as magic," Bobby said. He was the hardheaded realist of the family.

Emily squirmed in her chair. She and Bobby were like two cats rubbing each other the wrong way. "There is so magic." She turned to Papa as the highest authority. "Isn't there, Papa?"

Papa smiled at her indulgently. "Strange things do happen," he agreed, and then added slyly, "If you really want to find magic, it's all over China."

If I hadn't known better, I would have said he was almost jealous of our interest in Miss Lucy's book.

He coaxed. "You really need to learn more about China before you go there."

Bobby and I exchanged glances. Emily rolled her eyes. Not that China thing again. If it meant going there, I hoped we never got rich.

"Don't you want to hear Papa's story?" Mama urged.

"This isn't another story about Master Kung?" Emily asked cautiously. Master Kung was the Chinese name for the philosopher Americans called Confucius.

"No, no, this story goes back even further," Papa said quickly, as if he were afraid of losing his audience. Then he began, "The ancient books say that dream souls can go to the back of beyond."

Emily raised a bit of ham with her chopsticks. "Where's that?" she asked as she bit into it.

Papa sipped from a cup of tea. "It's very far away, farther even than China. I once read about a farmer's daughter who went there."

Everyone at the table was listening intently now.

Papa seemed relieved to have us listening. "When the farmer lost his wife, his daughter ran the whole household even though she was very young. Even so, the farmer wanted a mother for his daughter, so he married a neighbor woman."

> At first she was all smiles and sweet talk; but when the farmer died, the stepmother turned mean.
>
> She made her stepdaughter work all day and sleep with the animals at night.
>
> Though the girl did the work of two men, her stepmother would call her a lazy cow and beat her to work even harder. And when her stepmother broke the stick on the girl's back, she made the girl cut another stick so she could continue.
>
> One evening, when the stepmother had beat the girl especially hard, the girl felt as if she had torn muscles in her sides and back. When she heard a thud, she turned around and saw herself on the ground; she seemed to be standing beside her own body. She had become just her dream soul now.
>
> Of course, the stepmother could not see her dream soul. The girl was so happy that she gave a little hop—and wound up jumping to the top of the roof instead.
>
> Beneath her, her stepmother gave her body a

final kick and went in to dinner. Though it was now safe to return to her body, the orphan did not want to. This was the first time since her mother's death she had ever felt free.

"What happened?" Emily demanded.

"Her dream soul left her body," Papa explained.

Emily chewed thoughtfully. "What's that, anyway?"

Papa held up two fingers. At heart he was a scholar who liked to teach. "The Chinese believe that we each have two souls instead of one, like westerners believe. When we go to sleep, one of the souls stays with the body while the other goes journeying."

"To other places?" Emily asked, sifting through the toppings on her rice for more meat.

"And maybe other magical worlds. Or maybe worlds that are almost like ours with people who look like us—except not quite." Papa warmed to the notion. "So maybe in one of those worlds we run a blacksmith shop instead of a laundry."

"Or maybe there's no Bobby," Emily muttered. There was nothing but vegetables on her rice now, so she began to eye the bowl filled with the topping.

I leaned over and tapped my chopsticks on the rim of her bowl. "Eat your vegetables first before you go back into the big bowl." In a lower voice I warned her, "And don't let Mama hear you talking like that."

Emily chewed a vegetable slowly. "If I could see all those different places, I don't think I'd like to come back after just one evening."

Papa patted the table approvingly. "That's what happened. Because suddenly the girl heard a voice from far away, 'Come to me up here.'"

With another leap she soared upward higher and higher, until she saw a giant star. To her surprise, the star was sobbing.

"Why are you sad?" the girl wondered.

"I weep for you, child," the star said. "Every night in my travels I see such terrible things, but you suffer the worst. Let me grant your greatest wish. What do you most want?"

"For my father to be alive," the girl said.

The star gave itself a little shake. "Ask for something I can give," it said, and then warned, "But be careful what you wish. You just might get it."

"For my stepmother to be happy," the girl said.

"Nothing for yourself?" the star asked, puzzled.

"If she's happy, then I can be happy," the girl said.

"Then hurry," the star said. "Gather up my tears."

Wondering, the girl drew closer until she saw the drops falling from the eyes of the star. Stretching out a hand, she touched one, but it was cold and hard rather than wet. Picking it from the star's face, she saw that it was all shiny.

Thinking they were very pretty, she began to gather the tears and put them into her mouth.

"Now go," the star said, "before the sun rises."

Though there were more tears on the star's face, the girl waved good-bye and flew away in the lightening sky. But she got lost and couldn't find her way home.

In the meantime, her stepmother had found the girl's body still lying in the dirt. She tried everything to wake her up; and when she couldn't, she fetched a wisewoman from the village.

"This lazybones won't get up no matter what I do," the stepmother said in disgust. "She's getting way behind in her chores."

"Her dream soul got lost," the wise old woman said. "Get a piece of her clothing."

So the old stepmother got the girl's spare blouse and handed it to the wise old woman, who started to call her lost soul back to her.

Now the girl, lost among the worlds, heard the old woman from far away. Following the old woman's voice, she found her way back to the farmyard.

"Come back, come back," the old woman said, and put the blouse next to the girl's body.

Immediately the girl felt something tugging her toward the ground.

So she slipped into her body. The flesh seemed to clamp onto her like wet paste, and suddenly the world was black. She was beginning to use her body's senses.

The next moment she opened her eyes and sat up.

"Are you all right?" asked the wise old woman.

The girl tried to say something, but when she opened her mouth, the star's tears fell from her lips to the ground. Her stepmother picked one up and exclaimed, "Diamonds! Where did you get them?"

The girl told her, and the stepmother became very greedy. "Can you take me to that star?"

"I can try," the girl said. "But first you have to learn how to leave your body. It's like trying to get up without getting up."

So the stepmother took the diamonds, but she left the girl alone; and that evening they lay down together in the house.

However, when nothing happened, the stepmother became so angry that she grabbed a stick. "Liar!" She tried to beat the girl, but the girl ran outside. The stepmother chased her but then tripped over a rock and hit her head against the ground.

As she lay there unconscious, she heard the star crying from far away. "Where are you, child? Why haven't you visited me?"

The woman's dream soul rose with an odd, tearing sensation. When she saw her own body asleep, she became frightened. But her greed was stronger than her fear, so she picked up a sack as large as herself and flew fast and straight to where the great star was calling.

The star frowned when it saw the stepmother. "Who are you?"

On her flight to the star the stepmother had worked out her story. "The girl who was here got rich and left. I was hired to take her place. I'm an orphan who has led a hard life."

"Humph, well, you look pretty well fed," the star said.

"But it's all chaff and weeds," the stepmother insisted.

Now the star felt sorry for her, and so it said, "Very well. What do you most want?" It added, "But be careful what you wish. You just might get it."

"I want all your tears," the greedy woman said. And opening her huge sack, she began plucking the tears from the star.

When she had filled up half the sack, the star warned, "That's enough. The sun will be rising soon."

"But my sack's not full yet," the woman complained. "I want to be richer than the emperor."

Each time the star told her to go, she refused, insisting that her sack was not full enough.

So she was still gathering tears when the sun rose. Immediately the mean old stepmother burned up, and all that was left was a cloud of rusty smoke.

Papa's hand rose in the air as if it were a puff of smoke. "So watch out when you wish for something like

Christmas. You may not like what you get."

"But what about the girl, Papa?" Emily prompted.

Papa shrugged. "She sold her diamonds and lived happily ever after."

Excited, Emily set her bowl down. "I'm going to see if I can dream of a star tonight."

"What kind of hard life have you had?" Mama asked indignantly.

Emily glanced at Bobby. "Hard enough. Ow."

I ignored the glare Emily gave me after my warning pinch. "That was lovely, Papa."

Papa was pleased. "Almost as good as Miss Lucy's storybook?"

"Yes," Bobby said. "Are there any other ways to get rich?"

"There are plenty of stories," Papa boasted. "And they're all in my books. All you have to do is learn to read Chinese better. After all, we're going back there."

Papa was always trying to get us to learn more Chinese, but so far we had managed to get out of lessons. Even if we didn't have enough work already from our American classes, we had no intention of learning about a country we did not want to see. America was home.

When none of us leaped at Papa's offer, he picked up his bowl and used it to nudge Emily. "I thought you were curious about the old stories," he coaxed hopefully.

It didn't work. Emily squirmed. "Sure," she said. "Maybe after I make my pineapple."

My ears stood up at that. "Pineapple?"

"We're studying the states and territories in geography. I have to bring a product of Hawaii," Emily explained. "What does a pineapple look like?"

I drew one crudely on a piece of scrap paper. "Like that." Knowing my sister as well as I did, I was suspicious. "When do you have to have it?"

"The day after tomorrow," Emily said calmly. "I want to make a big pineapple out of papier-mâché." She spread her arms out as wide as she could to illustrate. "So we all have to get started right away."

"You need to give us more time," Mama scolded. By "us" she meant me.

Emily tried to defend herself. "Janey is doing Indiana. She's got to do a whole pig. At least I chose something without legs."

Papa looked around in puzzlement. "I just don't understand you children. There are so many wonderful stories."

We just sat stone-faced. It was the safest way.

"Well"—he sighed wistfully—"my books are always there when you want to look at them."

Not if we could help it.

four

When Mama opened the door, a puff of steamy air, warm and inviting, wafted into the bedroom. *"Time for school! Time to get up!"* She liked to practice her English.

"Yes, Mama." I was the first to get up. On the other side of the wall, in his room, I heard Bobby groan.

"I'm a caterpillar." Emily rolled our quilt around her like a cocoon.

I knew that game all too well. "Butterfly time," I announced, and dangled the wool stockings before her nose.

Emily's voice came muffled through the quilt that covered her mouth. "They itch."

"It's better to itch than have your legs get frostbitten and drop off." I draped the stockings over the top of her head.

Bobby knew his slowpoke sister as well as I did. "Is Emily up?" he asked through the wall.

"What do you think?" I shouted back.

"Remember what you told Papa," Bobby told her. "Remember Christmas."

At this rate, we would lose Christmas after less than twenty-four hours of the contest.

"I forgot." Emily grabbed her stockings, threw off the quilt and reached for her clothes.

"Hurry," Mama called from downstairs. "You're going to be late."

"Maybe our deal wasn't such a good idea after all," Emily said, dressing quickly. She even managed to get the stockings straight this time.

I started to put her shoes on. "Papa may have outsmarted us with that deal."

By the time we were finished, Bobby was almost hopping up and down in the doorway. "We're going to lose the bet and it hasn't even been one day," he said in disgust. "What's taking you so long?"

"You don't have to put on wool stockings." I glanced at the windup clock on the dresser. We might just make it. "Hurry."

We thundered down the steps and into the kitchen, but Mama wasn't there. Instead, her voice floated in from the front counter. "You'll have to make your own breakfasts and lunches." She must already be waiting on a customer.

I knew it was going to have be one of those hungry days. "We don't have time, Mama," I called to her.

Papa appeared from the hot drying room with a parcel wrapped in blue paper tucked under one arm. In his other hand, he had a glass of milk, which he raised in a toast. "There's always time to eat."

Hurriedly I made sandwiches for lunch, wrapped them in clean rags and put them into our lunch bags. In the meantime Bobby and Emily prepared porridge. It was undercooked in one part and scorched in the other, but we wolfed it down.

"Did you dream about weeping stars?" Bobby asked Emily.

"No," Emily said. "Did you?"

"Nope. That's why I'm going to go to school," Bobby said. "Then I'll get smart and make lots of money and buy a car like Mr. Barrington."

Picking up our galoshes from the newspaper-covered spot near the door, we sat on the kitchen chairs and went through the laborious process of putting them on over our shoes. Bobby was first as usual.

"Oof," I grunted as I tried to jam one of the galoshes over Emily's foot. "What did your feet do? Get a size bigger overnight?"

By tugging and shoving, we managed to get Emily's galoshes over her feet, and then I quickly did mine. Dressed in her muffler and coat and vests, Emily waddled almost like a penguin, and I felt like a knight wrapped in rubber and wool rather than steel.

When we finally stepped outside into the little courtyard in back, we found another inch of snow covering the ground. Across the way was Miss Lucy's small house. The window in her kitchen was brightly lit, as usual.

As we made our way down an alley to the front, we could hear laughter. Quickening our steps, we found two men standing outside our laundry, smiling and pointing.

"You ought to make it out of yellow snow," a fat man said. It was Sidney Skags, who had never liked the idea of having us in town.

To our horror, we saw that someone had vandalized our snowlady. Paper had been folded into a wide-based cone that looked vaguely like a coolie hat and placed on her, and the eyes had been rearranged so that the coal formed a slant. Even the coal mouth had been changed into a frown. They had a hung a rope from the back of the head to look like a queue.

It crossed my mind that Sidney might have been the vandal; but I dismissed the notion, because making a hat required work, and as Miss Lucy had once said, he had been on a permanent vacation since he had been born.

"They spoiled it," Emily said angrily, "those . . . those *Bull Moosers.*"

It was the worst insult Miss Lucy used, and we were convinced it meant something terrible, though for a long time none of us could figure out what. Maybe because of that, it had become our favorite swear word. Then, in American history class, I had heard about how Teddy Roosevelt had left the Republican party and started his own independent party, called the Bull Moose party. However, that only raised the question of why Miss Lucy would think calling someone a rogue Republican could be an insult.

I knocked the hat off the snowwoman and then yanked the queue away. "Some people can't leave anything in peace." I heard snickering in the crowd that was now gathering.

The snowman and snowwoman were beyond

correction for Emily. "They've been poisoned." She took her lunch bag and began swinging it at first one head and then the other.

"That's enough," I said when both heads were demolished, but Emily pulled free from my grasp and tried to shove over one of the snowpeople. When her muscles proved inadequate, she threw herself at it to knock it over.

The commotion had drawn Mama to the front doorway of the laundry. "What's wrong?"

Now almost as white as the snow herself, Emily whipped the rope from the ground. "Somebody hung this like a queue on our snowwoman."

"A queue?" Without his muffler or armor of clothing layers, Papa charged out of the house, his breath rising in angry plumes like steam rising from a ship's engine.

While I stared in surprise to see him in just his shirt, he nudged the rope as if it were a dead snake.

"A queue." Papa kicked it angrily. "Is this the Christmas spirit you say westerners practice?"

Despite the large group of friends and acquaintances who made us feel welcome now, there were still a few like Sidney who made no secret of their wish for us to move. We had withstood their insults since we had moved to town, so I couldn't understand why this particular one upset Papa so much that he would risk coming outside in the cold.

Emily kicked at the hat. "And those *Bull Moosers* put that on the head of my lady."

Mama usually kept a close check on our English by asking about new words. For once, though, she was too upset to bother. "You're getting covered with snow," Mama objected, and pulled her away. "Don't worry. I'll help you make new snowpeople."

I was all too aware of the growing crowd of passers-by around us. I was afraid at first. However, their faces weren't hostile. They were just curious and amused.

"Maybe it's better if we don't make any," I said. "It gives a certain element too many opportunities to mock us."

Mama didn't enjoy being the center of the spectacle. "Yes, maybe we shouldn't."

Papa gave the queue another kick and then faced the spectators. "*What wrong with you people?*"

I thought I heard Sidney's voice at the rear of the group. "*We ain't the strange ones.*"

People may have stopped out of curiosity, but suddenly they looked uncomfortable. They drifted away from Sidney as if they didn't want to be associated with him. No one spoke up, though. Most of the town was afraid of him and his pals, so I couldn't blame the onlookers.

Papa jabbed an index finger at him. "*I am not you. I am me. I no slave no more. I not wear queue. I free. I modern.*"

Sidney balled a hand into a big fist. "*But how much of a man are you?*" he challenged.

Papa looked mad enough to find out. Afraid, I fibbed: "*Better run, Sidney. I see the sheriff.*"

Sidney didn't even bother checking. He looked to his left, and since that seemed safe, he headed that way immediately. His friend plunged after him. And the rest of the crowd dispersed almost as quickly.

I tried to coax my father back inside. "Please, Papa," I begged quietly. "Don't make such a fuss. They were only snowpeople."

For a moment I saw the same wistful look on his face he had worn last night when he had tried to tell us about China. However, it was almost as if he was afraid we were going to try to ignore him once again. "You're Americans too. Just go," he sighed. "I'll do this myself."

"What, Papa?" I asked.

Papa didn't seem to hear me as he bent and picked up the rope and hat with his bare hands. "Bobby, throw those things away."

"Yes, Papa." Bobby gingerly took the rope and hat from him and went around to the back.

Bending again sadly, Papa began to roll the snow into a ball.

"What are you doing, Papa?" Emily asked.

"Rebuilding your snowpeople," Papa said. For him, though, making the snowpeople seemed like work, not play.

"But you hate snow, Papa," I said.

"I hate bullies more," he grunted.

We had never seen Papa get so upset before—let alone seen him touch snow willingly. Instinctively, we pressed in close to Mama.

She put her arms around us. "Tell the children. They don't understand."

Papa did not bother looking up. "They don't want to hear. They never do."

It took me a moment to find my voice. "Please, Papa."

Papa went on rolling the snowball bigger and bigger. "I will never wear a queue again. Nor will Bobby. The Manchus made all the Chinese men braid their hair in queues when they ruled China because it represented the tails of the horses they rode when they conquered us. When we finally got rid of the Manchus, we got rid of the queues too. We are no longer their slaves. And no one will make us wear the symbols of slaves again."

"Or our snowpeople?" Emily asked.

Papa was firm. "Not them either." He did his best to keep his voice even, but his frustration was plain. "We can't let bullies do this to us either in China or here. If we let them get away with small things, they'll get the courage to try bigger things."

"Come on," Mama whispered to us, bending to pick up snow.

As far as I was concerned, China was a million miles away. To me, China was only something my parents brought up when they wanted to criticize life here. I had decided long ago that what had happened back there didn't mean anything to me here. I was just as American as anyone else. And I certainly didn't think it was worth making a greater spectacle of ourselves. Why couldn't Papa try to fit in better to America?

"But we have school, Mama," I objected.

"You can write out a note and I'll sign it. Let's all help

your father." Mama released Emily and bent down to roll up more snow into a big ball.

Papa moved in a deliberate rhythm, taking little pleasure in the task; and we were so surprised by Papa's anger that none of us stopped to enjoy the moment of doing something together as a family.

When I thought it was safe, I sent Emily in to get coats and mittens for Papa and Mama; but though Mama put hers on gratefully, Papa left his on the doorstep. He worked with a steady fury, ignoring the cold for once.

"Aren't you coming to school, Joan?" Bernice asked.

Even without glimpsing the blaze of red hair, I would have known my friend. She had the straightest posture of any girl in town.

Bernice came from a vaudeville family that had actually been booked in theaters—though Bernice had yearned for a quiet, settled life and quit. I thought Bernice was fascinating because of her show-business history; but the more proper girls shunned her. In the town's opinion, actors were little better than thieves. In part, Bernice's careful diction, grammar and posture were attempts to distance herself from her past as an entertainer in vaudeville.

I felt my cheeks growing as red as her hair. *"I'll leave in a moment,"* I said.

With her were the blond-haired Havana and the brunette Henrietta, who was as short as Havana was tall. In fact, around the school they were called "the long and the short of it."

"We can't wait," Henrietta said fretfully, *"or we'll*

miss Jimmy Wilks." Henrietta was always reading romance magazines. She had a crush on a different boy in school each day. Today her heart was set on Jimmy. Tomorrow, who knew.

"It's all right. You go on," I urged her.

A small girl came up then. She was my friend Florie, and she started to pull some magazines from her book bag. *"I was going to give you these at school, but why don't you take them now? Then you won't have to lug them home."*

To my mortification, Mama answered for me. *"Leave Joan alone,"* she said.

I found it almost painful to be a public spectacle like this, so I rolled my eyes meaningfully at my father. *"I'm sorry. I'll see you later."*

Bernice, who had a quirky family of her own, nodded. *"Let's go,"* she said to the others.

If ever there were two more joyless snowpeople made, I can't think of them.

Afterward Papa retreated to his study to calm himself down by writing a poem. "Make me a cup of tea, please," he asked Mama.

"I'll warm some milk for you," Mama said. "It's better for you." Miss Lucy had preached the benefits of drinking milk to the point where Mama had become convinced it would help cure most anything.

While Mama warmed the milk, I wrote out two notes, one for Bobby and Emily and one for me. Then, with great care, Mama signed her name the way Miss Lucy had shown her. "There," she said, and she laid the pencil down.

"Very good, Mama," I said.

She beamed proudly as she admired her handiwork. "*Practice makes perfect,*" she said, quoting one of Miss Lucy's favorite proverbs.

A glance at the clock told me that I would probably miss part of the first period, English. The next period was a test in history, which I did not want to miss. So when we were outside, I started slogging through the snow. The cold made me pant. "Come on. Let's take the shortcut."

Emily dawdled as usual. "I'm not in any hurry."

I seized her mittened hand. "The note doesn't explain missing the whole day." I was going to have a hard enough time from my principal about missing a class.

Emily pulled in the opposite direction. "Don't be so bossy."

Bobby resolved the stalemate by grabbing her coat collar and dragging her forward. "You're always making us late." While Bobby might not have cared particularly for school, he was the impatient sort who always liked to reach his destination as quickly as he could.

"Okay, okay." Emily shook free and stomped angrily along the track that the other children had beaten through the snow.

As hard as she pumped her little legs, it was easy to get ahead of her with a few long strides. "Wait," I said.

While it was fine to let Emily lead along a well-trodden path, I knew that I had to break a trail through our shortcut. The snow lay up to mid calf, and once I plunged all the way up to my knees.

When we reached the first fence, the snow on the rails lay as thick as Miss Lucy's vanilla icing. Bobby eased up beside me. Cautious as two dough boys in no-man's-land, we crouched and peered between the slats. "I don't see anyone, do you?"

I looked through the space between the slats and felt Emily next to me, peering through a lower one. "No." In the spring and summer there was a sea of furry-headed wheat, but now the field lay quiet as a frozen sea of milk. I saw about a half dozen different furrows across the undulating surface, so I knew that others had taken the shortcut as well. The furrows led over the field to the opposite side, where the ground sloped upward to the top of the hill where our schools sat. A second fence ran like a length of stitches across the middle of the slope.

Farmer Pynchon's barn was just a bulky white block on the horizon, and his house was hardly more than a chip. Smoke rose from it, rising in a leisurely worm toward the gray sky.

"Let's go," Bobby said impatiently. "I don't smell Farmer Pynchon around. He always smokes a cheap stogie. On a clear cold day like today, you can whiff him from a mile away."

"Only if he's upwind," I warned.

However, Bobby had already thrown his lunch over, and then his schoolbooks, bound by a leather strap.

"Come on, let's go." Bobby surged up the fence railings.

Emily and I threw our books and lunches over the fence; it was a little awkward for me because I was taller and in a skirt, but I managed to climb over the railings and then down into the field.

"Joanie, wait," Emily called.

"Shh," I whispered, and turned back. Emily lay with her belly on the lower railing as she raised her legs. With a lunge, she fell feetfirst off the railing and into the field.

"Now don't argue with me. Walk in my footsteps." I spoke softly, afraid that Farmer Pynchon would hear us even at this distance.

"Bobby," Emily said in a low voice.

True to his hasty nature, Bobby had already begun to plow his way across the snow, heedless of me or Emily. "Quiet," he whispered back.

Seizing Emily's mittened hand, I began to pull her after me.

Bobby was already ten paces ahead and widening the gap. I shuffled forward, breaking a trail for Emily behind me. "Bobby, wait up."

"I'm tired of waiting," he said without looking back.

I angled across the field until I reached his track. That made the going a lot easier, and soon Emily and I were dogging his steps.

We had gone about three quarters of the way across the field when we heard Farmer Pynchon's voice cut through the still, cold air. It was a voice strengthened and hardened by decades as an auctioneer. *"Hey, you kids. Get out of my field."*

I couldn't help looking over my shoulder. He was like a black bug in the distance, but I saw twin plumes of steam. "He must be riding a horse," I said.

With one thought we plunged forward. Bobby led the way, and Emily and I followed. As long as we were on the level field, we were all right, but the trouble began when we reached the slope. Bobby battled through the snow, but the slope was so steep that our feet began to slip.

"Wait, Joanie," Emily complained. There was a new ragged edge to her voice that caught my attention.

I turned. "You have to keep up," I told her.

"I . . . I'm trying," she gasped, and slipped even as I watched.

I let go of her hand so I wouldn't yank her arm out of its socket. Farmer Pynchon sounded closer, and I looked back. I could see that he was definitely riding a horse—probably his old bay mare. *"I'll fix you,"* he was yelling.

As she knelt in the snow, Emily had also glanced at the field. Now she faced me again and held up a mittened hand in noble farewell. "Save yourself."

"You've been seeing too many movies at the nickelodeon," I said, and got behind her. *"Upsy daisy."* Hooking my hands underneath her arms, I jerked her to her feet.

Bobby, too, had made his way back to us. "Come on, lump," he grumbled good-naturedly, and took her wrist.

As I began to push from behind, Bobby began to pull from in front. "Oof. If we're going to do this again, you're going to have to cut out the desserts."

Emily tried to move her short legs as quickly as she could, but mostly it was like shoving a woolen boulder up the hill. By the time we reached the fence, I could hear the farmer's horse snorting.

"I see you. I know who you are. It ain't gonna end here," the farmer warned.

Bobby slid easily through the fence and turned to help Emily. I didn't even bother with the niceties but simply picked her up and passed her between the railings to

Bobby, who helped set her on her feet.

Then I turned sideways to climb on through. *"I'm sorry,"* I said to the farmer. *"But we were late."*

Farmer Pynchon was a heavy man who sat like a sack of potatoes on top of his horse. On his head was a fur hat with flaps that he had tied together beneath his unshaven chin. *"Then start earlier,"* he snapped. *"See here. I don't want you kids tromping around. I'm tired of it, you hear?"*

That might have been true during a thaw, when the ground turned muddy, but right now it looked pretty frozen to me. However, I didn't think it would help any to point that out. *"We weren't the only ones,"* I said as I went through.

"And that's the whole point," the farmer growled. *"If your folks won't teach you to respect my property, I'll give you a lesson you won't forget."*

On the other side Bobby had finished brushing the snow from Emily. *"We're sorry, sir,"* I said. *"It won't happen again."*

"You bet it won't," he hinted darkly.

Having climbed over the second fence, we were now halfway up the slope, again at the road that curled around Farmer Pynchon's property.

As we began to make our way up the road to the hilltop, he shouted after us. *"Don't ever trespass again."*

"There goes Christmas." Emily sighed. "And there go our presents."

five 

"Excuse me, neighbors," a man said.

All of us stopped. We had been so busy arguing that we had not noticed Mr. Barrington's sleek automobile, which had pulled up to the curb.

James Barrington raised his hat. *"Could you direct us to the high school?"*

"Yes," I said, and was about to point when I received a sudden inspiration. *"In fact, I'm going there right now."*

"Wizard!" Victoria said in delight.

Emily was already heading toward the car. *"We'd better hurry,"* she reminded me.

"Hop in then," Mr. Barrington said. At his nod Victoria opened the door to the back of the car.

Excitedly we piled in. I did my best to seem calm, because I did not want to seem like some rube. However, much to my chagrin, Emily announced, *"This is our first ride in a car."*

To my relief, though, Mr. Barrington did not laugh. *"I'm honored,"* he said with a little bow.

Bobby was caressing the metal of the door. *"How big is the engine?"*

"Let's find out, shall we?" When he winked, Mr. Barrington looked like a small boy in the same club as Bobby. As he stretched his hands to grip the steering wheel, he exposed the sleeve cuffs. They both seemed fine. So I figured that as usual Mama had been finding fault where there wasn't any.

When Mr. Barrington released the hand brake and set the car in motion, exhaust plumed from behind the car as we swung back out into the street. The sudden acceleration threw us against the leather-upholstered backseat.

The grammar school seemed to leap at the powerful car. *"Would you let my brother and sister off here?"* I blurted out.

With the quick reactions of a fighter pilot, Mr. Barrington jammed on the brake and released the clutch. The car screeched as its tail wriggled back and forth on the icy street and then righted itself.

I thought he would be annoyed, but instead he calmly pulled over to the curb. *"Of course,"* he said.

"Tell them that you were helping a new student find her school," I whispered to Bobby in Chinese.

"Got you," he said with a wink. Opening the rear door, he slid out and onto the street, where he gave the automobile one last, affectionate look.

Emily started to slide across the seat after him, her hands caressing the leather wonderingly. She paused with her legs halfway out the door. *"Ta-ta. We really must do this again sometime,"* she declared.

She must have been getting at some of the high-toned society magazines I had borrowed from my friend Florie. *"Emily,"* I scolded her.

However, Mr. Barrington gave her a dazzling smile. "*Yes, we must.*"

"See?" Emily said triumphantly to me.

"Come on, lump." Grabbing her wrist, Bobby jerked her out of the car.

"The high school is just beyond the grammar school," I said, pointing.

"Goodness, we could have walked," Victoria said.

"Except we would be late." I pointed at the imposing woman standing on the top step just before the school doors. *"That's the principal, Miss Blake. She hates tardiness."*

Mr. Barrington stroked first the left side of his mustache and then the right as if it were a miniature pet. *"Does she? You just leave her to me, then."* He sounded as if he enjoyed the challenge.

Gunning the motor, he raced the hundred yards to the high school and pulled up to the curb. With boyish energy he leaped out of the car and ran around to open first Victoria's car door and then mine. *"Ladies,"* he said.

I was so dazed by the whole experience that I trailed them into the school yard and up the steps where Miss Blake stood, holding the bell by its clapper so that her hand was hidden inside. It made her look like some pirate queen with a dagger for one hand.

"Miss Blake? I believe we spoke on the telephone.

How do you do?" Giving her one of his dazzling smiles, he bounced up the steps with an outstretched hand. *"I'm James Barrington."*

Even a hardened veteran like Miss Blake found it impossible to resist his overwhelming charm. Shifting the bell to her other hand, she shook his. *"Hello."*

Mr. Barrington turned and waved a hand toward me. *"We were like two lost lambs until we met Joan. I'm afraid we've made her late. She's such an angel. It speaks well of Joan's mentors."* He indicated his daughter. *"I can rest easy, knowing that my daughter, Victoria, is in good hands."*

Miss Blake seemed dazed for a moment. *"Unh . . . yes, well, come with me to my office and we'll register her."* Miss Blake turned. *"You come too, Joan. You can guide Victoria to her first class."*

As we passed, Mr. Barrington whispered to me, *"You see, Joan? When I'm around, no good deed will go unrewarded."*

I tried to think of something smart and funny, but all I could manage was a pedestrian, *"Thank you."*

We followed Miss Blake down the hallway with its brown linoleum floor and gray walls. Once we were inside the office, Mr. Barrington held out his hands to his daughter. *"My dear?"*

When Victoria turned her back, I saw that her coat was flared like the latest ones in Florie Adams' fashion magazines. It was the color they call Japan blue. Scarlet silk had been stitched in stripes around the cuffs and below the waist.

To my surprise Victoria shrugged her coat into her father's hands. It had a pale-blue silk lining, but the lining wasn't the reason that I stared.

I had seen women helped off with their coats, but never a girl my own age. It was a small thing, I knew, but it was obvious that he thought of his daughter as someone very special. And they carried out their parts in the ritual with such well-practiced assurance that I assumed they had performed it many times before.

Draping her coat over his arm for the moment, he held out his hand. She gave a half curtsy as she lifted her hat.

And then I really stared—not because her hair was colored a coppery red but because it was so short. Bobby's hair was longer. From Florie's magazines, I knew her hairdo was "bobbed" with a swirl of curls called a "marcel." It was the kind of hairstyle that women wore in the fast movies that I was not allowed to view—except, of course, in the articles in Florie's magazines. I had never expected to see that haircut in person—and certainly never on a girl my own age. It seemed . . . well . . . scandalous.

As Miss Blake and I gazed at her, Victoria seemed amused. She felt the back of her head playfully. *"Oh dear. Is it too long?"*

Miss Blake found her voice first. *"In fact, you might think of letting it grow longer,"* she hinted.

Mr. Barrington sprang immediately to his daughter's defense. *"Is there some code about hair length? Must all students wear their hair long, including the boys?"*

Miss Blake hesitated while she tried to run through

the rules mentally. "*Well . . . no. Not exactly.*"

"*Then thank you so much for not making a fuss,*" Mr. Barrington said with a slight nod.

Miss Blake looked confused. "*Yes, of course. You're welcome,*" she said uncertainly.

Marveling at Mr. Barrington's verbal footwork, I started to take off my coat, Mr. Barrington swung around. "*Allow me.*" I felt his hand take my coat collar, and then he gently drew it back, helping me off with my coat.

Mr. Barrington seemed to turn everything into a game as he dipped his head and hung both his daughter's coat and mine on wall pegs, and then his.

Miss Blake dug into a pile of papers. "*Where did you go to school before, Victoria?*"

Mr. Barrington answered for her. "*Oh, here and there,*" he said breezily. He dug an envelope out of his coat and presented it to Miss Blake. "*You'll find all the details in there.*"

When he drew a chair back for his daughter to sit down, I suddenly felt terribly jealous of her. He seemed so considerate and attentive that my father seemed . . . well . . . foreign. Almost immediately, I felt ashamed of myself.

Miss Blake's eyebrows rose. "*London, Geneva?*" She looked at Victoria. "*You've traveled quite far for one so young.*

"*But,*" she persisted, "*after London and Geneva, Clarksburg must be a letdown.*" Left unasked was what had brought the Barringtons here.

Victoria was as gracious as her father. "*After having lived abroad, I think it's nice to return to your homeland.*"

Mr. Barrington dropped into a second chair. "*My dear Miss Blake, Clarksburg can seem as exotic as Geneva if you've never seen it but only heard about it through your father's stories.*"

Miss Blake selected a pencil from a cup in front of her. "*I really couldn't say, Mr. Barrington—having never traveled out of state in my life.*"

"*Then London is the poorer for never having been graced by your presence, Miss Blake.*" Mr. Barrington's teeth seemed perfect when he smiled.

Miss Blake raised her pencil in surrender. "*You can turn off the charm, Mr. Barrington. I don't have any money to invest in Florida swampland or whatever you have for sale.*"

Mr. Barrington clasped his chest as if wounded. And I decided then that he wasn't so much playing a game as acting a part—and to his great delight he knew he had the lead role. "*Miss Blake, you cut me to the quick.*"

The corners of her mouth twitching up a smile, Miss Blake began to write. "*But if I did have money, I'd probably wind up giving you every penny of it.*"

The only difficulty came when Miss Blake asked Mr. Barrington for his occupation. "*Ah, well,*" he said with an annoyed shrug, "*I'm looking at various opportunities.*" It seemed to be a sore point.

Miss Blake's pencil hovered over the form. "*I need to put something down.*"

Victoria glanced mischievously at her father and then suggested to Miss Blake, "*Whatever Father does, he will always be a gentleman.*"

Mr. Barrington bowed. "*Thank you, my dear.*"

Victoria graciously nodded back.

I studied Victoria while her father and Miss Blake filled out the rest of the forms. She was wearing a frock of navy-blue velveteen with shirring at the low waistline that was accented by side-tie sashes. The collar was hand embroidered with silk of many colors in a geometric pattern. In my regular dress I felt shabby and dowdy by comparison.

By the time they were finished, I had worked myself into a serious fit of shyness. When Miss Blake gave Victoria her schedule of classes, I saw that we would have several together.

That done, Mr. Barrington sprang to his feet while Victoria waited patiently for him to draw her chair back. When he had retrieved her hat and coat, he presented them to her. "*I'll pick you up after school, dear. I'll get our things out of storage so we can move in to Miss Bradshaw's.*" As he turned to get his own things, he grinned at me. "*And thank you so much for rescuing us in our hour of need, Joan. . . .*" He arched an eloquent eyebrow.

"*You're welcome.*" I caught myself before I went into a curtsy.

"*Well, Joan, I hope that you and Victoria will be good friends.*" He handed me my coat in turn.

When we had left the office and Victoria had said good-bye to her father, I hunted for something to say to such an exotic creature. "*I hope things won't be too tame compared to London.*"

One corner of her mouth curled up knowingly. "*Father always has a way of livening things up.*"

"I can't even imagine," I admitted truthfully. *"This way to English. We have it together."*

Victoria inclined her head slightly in acknowledgment. Most anyone, including me, would have been petrified the first day; but she carried herself with a regal assurance.

Nor did Victoria seem the least bit fazed at being the center of attention when our teacher, Mr. Stevens, had her introduce herself to the rest of the class. It was almost as if she were used to it—even bored.

As the daughter of the richest man in town, Ann Wood was used to speaking up when she wanted. The moment she saw Victoria's hairdo, she spoke to one of her friends in a mock whisper that was actually meant to carry through the classroom. *"Look at her. She seems a bit bohemian."*

Among ourselves my friends and I referred to Ann and her snooty circle as the flock because they were like so many pigeons cooing to one another as they preened. They laughed now with Ann.

Victoria smiled sweetly at Ann. *"If you mean am I from Bohemia, no; but I have been in Prague."*

Ann was using "bohemian" in the way most people did: as a term for someone who lived a little fast and a little shabbily. However, that description didn't exactly apply to Victoria's clothes.

When she finally looked down from Victoria's hair to her expensive frock, Ann Wood drew her eyebrows together as if she were thinking hard—it wasn't an expression her face wore often.

"Barrington. Didn't my father buy your bank?" she asked.

Victoria pretended to ignore Ann's rudeness. *"I believe my grandfather once owned a bank here before his business interests took him elsewhere."*

Since I had come in for my share of Ann's snubbing, I smiled at Victoria as she sat down.

Mr. Stevens frowned at Ann but did not reprimand her. Like most in the town, he owed money to her father. *"I'm sure the class will make you feel welcome, Victoria,"* he said, and picked up a book. *"Now, shall we begin today's discussion of Dickens'* Oliver Twist*?"* It was, of course, a rhetorical question. There was the usual thudding and clattering as we got out our books and opened them. In the meantime Mr. Stevens had raised his voice to be heard over the noise. *"Charles Dickens was writing about a time when England was experiencing immense changes due to the Industrial Revolution. London was growing by leaps and bounds."*

Victoria put up her hand and when Mr. Stevens acknowledged her, she said, *"It can still be quite confusing. There are all these narrow lanes and little byways. I had a tutor who was quite helpful."*

Mr. Stevens lowered his book. *"You've been to London, Victoria? I envy you."*

Victoria didn't so much tell us about London as bring it to life. Everyone, including Ann, began asking her questions about that city. I found myself envying not only her knowledge but her self-assurance. I had to assume that it was all her private tutors. I suppose all that individual attention was also what make her speak more like an adult as well.

It turned out that Victoria had been to many places that the rest of us only talked about seeing. Her travels gave Victoria a certain sophisticated aura that allowed Ann to overlook her hair. After class Ann and her flock surrounded poor Victoria. *"Let me show you how to use your locker,"* Ann said, and practically kidnapped the newcomer.

During the exam in the next period, the teacher got me to lend her my history book to read while the rest of us took the test. As I pondered an essay question, I glanced at her and saw her flipping through the pages idly, as if the history of England and France were old hat to her.

With Ann taking Victoria under her wing, I didn't have much to do. I lost sight of her for the next period, but at lunch I went over to her. *"I notice you don't have any lunch,"* I said. *"Would you like some of mine?"*

"Thank you. What is it?" she asked.

I had made the sandwiches myself that morning. *"Baloney."*

There were gales of laughter from Ann and her friends. *"What a tawdry little meal."*

Victoria frowned at Ann and then looked back at me. *"Ann's already offered to share hers with me. But why don't you sit with us?"* She glanced at Ann as a signal to make room, but Ann and her flock stayed glued to their spots on the bench.

The last thing in the world I wanted to do was sit with Ann. *"Th-that's all right. I just wanted to make sure you had something to eat."* I started to beat a hasty retreat.

My friend Bernice came to my rescue. *"Over here, Joan,"* she called.

Gratefully I headed for the haven of her bench. Havana and Henrietta were there too, and Henrietta pulled me down beside her. *"I saw you through the classroom window when you arrived. Who was that dreamy man who drove you here?"*

"He was her father," I said.

Next to them was Florie. Her black hair was pulled back into a bun and decorated with a red bow in honor of the season. *"Who cares about him? Did you see the new girl's clothes?"* she asked. She knew all about such things from her slick fashion magazines.

"But did you see her hair? My mother says that a woman's glory is her hair." Henrietta rolled her eyes.

"Well, there can't be much glory if there's not much hair." Florie giggled.

Henrietta sniffed. *"I think it makes her look so fast."*

Havana leaned in close to them. *"Did you see her eyes? So sad. I'm sure there must be something tragic in her life."* Havana came from a large family—most of whom seemed to be suffering from one calamity or another.

"She has the eyes of an actress," Bernice said in her usual crisp diction.

Florie studied Victoria. *"I guess we could see her in something at the nickelodeon."* Every Saturday she paid her nickel to see a serial and a movie.

From where we sat, we had been able to hear snatches of Victoria's conversation with Ann and her flock. I caught the names of London and Paris and Geneva. Ann had tried her best to match Victoria, but it was clear that all her knowledge came from magazines, while Victoria's came from firsthand experience.

Havana sighed. *"Someday,"* she swore, *"I'll see all those places the new girl talks about."*

"And you'll do it with your own money, too." Bernice sniffed.

I nudged my friend. *"Are you jealous?"*

"Who wouldn't be?" Florie said.

"She's nothing but a spoiled little princess like Ann," Bernice insisted.

Victoria was more than that, though. The surprise came in physical education class later that day. We were all outfitted in middy blouses and loose pants called bloomers, which sagged on our legs like deflated balloons.

We were in the gymnasium playing basketball. Girls' basketball was different from boys'. Each team had six players, and the court was divided into three parts with two guards, two centers and two forwards.

Ann and her flock all had letters from their doctors excusing them from playing; and since they were hopeless with the ball, our teacher, Miss Armstrong, let them stay on the sidelines. So I was surprised when Victoria trotted onto the court for the opposing team and took up a position opposite me in my part of the court. She looked good even in the silly bloomers we had to wear.

And I realized her short hair would be more practical than mine when we had to shower after gym class.

I was a guard for my team with tiny Henrietta, who tried to make up for her lack of height by hopping up and down continually like a jack-in-the-box. Havana was tall enough to win the tip-off at center court. I ran down the ball, dribbled once and pivoted to pass to Henrietta. (In girls' rules you were allowed to dribble only once before you had to pass or shoot.) However, a perfectly manicured hand appeared from nowhere and slapped the ball out of my hands. My palms still stinging from the blow, I lunged for it, but Victoria hipped me out of the way.

When Victoria bounce passed it to her teammate, Henrietta tried to intercept it but missed.

Victoria's teammate took a shot, but it bounced off the rim. With the litheness of a gazelle, Victoria sprang toward the basket and caught the rebound. I ran toward her, trying to put a hand in front of her face to distract her.

She almost made it seem like part of a ballet as she landed, pivoted on one foot and shot at the basket. It banked off the backboard and fell through the net.

Miss Armstrong blew her whistle. *"Two points!"*

Victoria caught the ball on the bounce and passed it to our teacher. As play carried it to the other basket, I went up to the boundary of our third of the court to wait for a pass. We were not allowed to go over the line.

Victoria took up her position next to me. The amazing thing was that she had not broken into a sweat.

"Where did you learn to play basketball? In Geneva?"

For a moment it was as if she dropped her royal mask, and I saw a deep sadness claim her face and eyes. *"Here and there,"* she answered enigmatically.

At the other basket her team managed to get the ball.

I got ready to intercept the pass. The basketball floated through the air, growing larger and larger until it seemed as big as an orange moon and impossible to miss. However, when I reached for it, I was left grasping only air; and the next thing I knew, Miss Armstrong was blowing her whistle. *"Two points!"*

I turned to see Victoria trotting back from the basket. *"I know you didn't learn that fake in Geneva."*

Victoria smiled as if I had paid her the greatest compliment. *"Thank you, but you're not bad yourself."*

"I haven't been able to guard you, though," I confessed.

A corner of her mouth twisted down with a savagery that surprised me, and her smile became bitter. *"We have quick feet in my family."*

"So do we, but it doesn't seem to be doing much good." I sighed.

On the court and dressed like everyone else, she seemed like a normal girl. Or rather, a normal girl who was also a superb athlete.

She scored twice more—each time she got her hands on the ball. Then Miss Armstrong was blowing her whistle for the next groups to replace us.

As soon as we jogged off, Ann and her flock closed around their champion. *"You were marvelous,"* Ann said enthusiastically.

Victoria gave me another apologetic smile, and then the royal mask had snapped back into place as she turned her back on me to concentrate on Ann.

six

When school was finished, I looked for Victoria. It wasn't easy to miss her, because she was standing by her car with Ann and her flock—who were busy admiring Mr. Barrington rather than his automobile.

When Victoria saw me, she whispered something to her father. "*Miss Lee.*" He doffed his hat. "*We're in need of a wilderness guide this afternoon.*"

Ann's flock parted away from me on either side as if they were afraid of some kind of contamination. It seemed to me that any of them knew the town far better than I did. "*Where do you need directions to?*"

Mr. Barrington took a deep breath and there were a half dozen pairs of eyes watching the rise and fall of his chest. "*I feel the need of some exercise. Can you direct us to a suitable hill for sledding?*"

"*There are a lot of hills to use for sledding,*" I said. It was my first snowfall in town, so I didn't know what the other children used.

Ann frowned. "*You don't need Joan's help. I know which one everyone uses for sledding.*"

"*A second opinion wouldn't hurt,*" Mr. Barrington said gently.

"*Shouldn't we move into our new place first?*" Victoria asked dutifully.

Mr. Barrington indicated Ann and her flock with his hat. "*How could we be cruel to your friends?*"

I tried to keep my mouth from dropping open, because I couldn't think of one other adult who would drop everything just to please his daughter.

Ann flung an arm up and pointed eagerly. "*The best place is only a quarter mile past town.*" I don't think even Ann could have gotten so much chauffeuring from her indulgent father.

"*How fortuitous.*" Mr. Barrington set his hat back on his head.

Victoria put a glove on his arm. "*But it might be rather late when we finish sledding.*" Victoria tried as hard to be a good daughter as I did.

Mr. Barrington waved his hand breezily. "*The moving men can work overtime.*" He wasn't about to pinch pennies when it came to his daughter's pleasure.

"*But won't that disturb Miss Bradshaw or the Lees?*" Victoria worried.

"*I'm sure they'll tell us if we do.*" Mr. Barrington turned that dazzling smile on me again. "*But won't you come with us now, Miss Lee? Our party won't be complete without you.*"

I stood there, embarrassed. I hated to be reminded of the difference between myself and my schoolmates. While the whole town would be enjoying the snow, I had my homework and my chores to do. And first I would have to go through the dreaded quiz.

"I'm sorry," I said, feeling my cheeks reddening. *"I'm afraid I can't."*

"I was so hoping you could," Victoria said.

Mr. Barrington sounded as disappointed as his daughter. *"A previous appointment?"*

Ann glanced at me sideways with a mocking smile. *"Everyone knows Joan isn't the friendly type."*

It was bad enough that I couldn't go, but it was adding insult to injury to have Ann remind me of my lack of social activities.

"I have homework and chores to do," I explained.

Mr. Barrington looked as if I had just said I had to fly to the moon. *"Surely books and chores can wait until later."* When he spoke, I knew the tug the children of Hamelin must have felt when they heard the Pied Piper begin to play his flute.

The fun-loving Mr. Barrington was such a contrast to Papa, who interrogated me about my friends to make sure they weren't robbers and murderers. And once Papa was sure that they weren't criminals, he lost interest in the topic.

"Unless you're ashamed to be seen in the company of an old fogy."

I got quite flustered. *"But you're not old. I mean you're not a fogy."* Quickly I corrected herself. *"I mean you're neither old nor a fogy."*

Mr. Barrington patted his heart mockingly. "*Reprieved.*"

"*Why don't you ask your parents if you can come with us?*" Victoria suggested.

It was almost like peeking into someone else's dream. And I wanted to go with them—wanted to go with them so badly that it hurt inside. But I knew my parents. They had a laundry to run. "*It's just impossible.*"

"*Pity, but perhaps some other time then.*" Mr. Barrington sighed. Recovering his good humor the next moment, he turned to the others. "*Ladies?*" he said as he opened the rear car door.

I stood there awkwardly as Ann and her flock piled into the car with Victoria. "*Would you like a lift, Joan?*"

"*That would be nice. The laundry's on your way,*" I said, starting to move toward the car.

"*There's no room,*" Ann said quickly.

I looked into the crowded car. It was quite true.

Mr. Barrington had been staring uncertainly around his car. "*I seem to have seriously overestimated the size of my vehicle. I do apologize, Joan.*"

Even so, Victoria tried to slide over in her seat. "*We'll make room somehow.*"

"*But we'll be so squeezed,*" Ann said, pouting.

Only Ann would have made the Barringtons choose between being polite to me or to her.

Mr. Barrington scratched his cheek forlornly. "*You do see our problem, don't you, Joan?*"

I guess it wasn't enough to be their future neighbor. Ann was really more of their class; and as nice as Mr.

Barrington was, I guess that counted for more. Beneath all his nice manners, he was a snob after all.

I felt bad for feeling bad. And yet I also felt resentful that Ann was pushing me out of the car. However, I could prove that I was bigger than her or Mr. Barrington. *"Of course,"* I said, *"I wouldn't want to inconvenience you."*

Mr. Barrington waved his hand apologetically. *"I'm sorry, Joan. Next time."*

Victoria turned as if she were going to say something, but then the automobile roared away.

"Don't you think Mr. Barrington has a swell car?" Bobby asked as he came over to me.

"It's all right," I said, pretending as if I didn't care.

"One of these days I'm going to have one—only bigger," Bobby said.

Emily slogged through the snow. The front of her coat was a mess. *"I like snow, but I hate slush."*

"What happened to you?" I asked as I tried to brush off her front.

"I got shoved into the street." She scowled.

"I saw it all. You slipped," Bobby said, laughing.

"That Andy pushed me," Emily growled.

I put on my best district-attorney frown as I quizzed her. *"And what did you say to him?"*

"I told him that if he wanted to make a Texas longhorn, he just had to stick a branch on either side of his head." She brushed at her coat clumsily. *"I'm glad I chose something easy like a pineapple."* Emily grew thoughtful. It was always a dangerous sign for somebody. *"Just wait till tomorrow. I'll fix Andy's wagon."*

"No, you won't." I switched to Chinese. "Remember your promise. Stay out of trouble until Christmas is over. Or we can't even think about asking for presents."

"But Andy will think I'm scared of him," Emily complained.

"We'll be in enough trouble if Papa finds out we cut through Farmer Pynchon's field. If you want to have Christmas this year, you have to change. It's only for a little while," I argued.

"All right," Emily grumped. "But I'm sure earning my present."

I couldn't help thinking of the Barringtons. I was sure that their Christmases must be as marvelous as their lives seemed to be; and that notion only made me feel sadder. And as we slogged down the hill, I knew I was getting tired of being different all the time.

Inside the laundry Papa was trying to explain something to a young man in his twenties. I recognized him as Harold. Though he worked as an automobile mechanic, he passed for fast company in our town, with hair slicked back so much that we often wondered whether he used brilliantine or the grease from his garage. In the parlance of Florie's faster magazines, he was a "jellybean."

Papa was already red in the face, as if the argument had been going on a long time. Lifting a pillowcase from a pile of dirty laundry, he shouted, *"Too dirty. Too dirty."* He flapped it in frustration at the young car mechanic.

Harold pulled at his collar. *"Hang it all, I know it's dirty. That's why I brung it in—so's you can clean it."*

When Papa heard the bell ring over the doorway, he turned to see it was us. Gratefully, Papa waved me toward him. Through his muffler, he said to me in Chinese, "Will you tell this man that I can't get out the pomade stains?"

When I was little, I used to envy my friends because their parents acted like real grown-ups and took care of everything. Because I spoke English while my father did not—and my mother spoke it poorly—mine had depended on me from an early age. I not only had to interpret for them but also frequently had to handle many unpleasant things for them, such as getting into the middle of arguments. I was embarrassed.

At the moment, I felt I was like the parent and my father the child I had to shield. *"Excuse me, sir,"* I said, trying to defuse the anger that the miscommunication had inadvertently created. *"I don't think we can get out those stains."*

Harold looked just as relieved to see me as Papa. *"Is that what's he's been jawing about for the last ten minutes?"*

It seemed all my life that I'd had to deal with American customers who had been infuriated accidentally by my father. Having dealt with storms like this before, I knew ultrapoliteness would chase the clouds away. *"He didn't mean any harm, sir,"* I said, smiling. *"My father prides himself on the quality of our work and wouldn't want to disappoint you."*

My flattery had its usual effect. Almost preening like a peacock, Harold waved for Papa to add the pillowcase to the pile. *"Well, do the best you can."*

When I translated for Papa, he grunted. "Tell him Thursday."

Having successfully played the peacemaker yet again, I

sorted through the items, writing out the ticket. *"They'll be ready Thursday. We'll try our best with the pillowcase."*

"See you then, kiddo," Harold said, taking his receipt. As he turned toward the street, I hurried past him so I could open the door for him. Stuffing his hands in his pockets, he nodded to me before he skipped airily down the steps.

Relieved, Papa sat on a stool and sipped from a glass of milk. I waited for a thank-you, or at least a "good job," but instead, Papa frowned. "Farmer Pynchon has been by."

Emily and Bobby and I looked at each other, but they left it up to me to venture, "How much laundry did he leave?"

Papa had a milk mustache. "He came to tell me you were trespassing on his land."

I tried not to laugh at Papa when so much was at stake, but his face was a comical sight. "But everyone does it when they're late."

Papa wagged a finger back and forth. "I don't care if the American children don't respect other people's property. I expect you to."

"But it's wintertime. The ground's frozen solid," I argued.

"It would be wise to stay away," Papa said firmly. "He's a man with a strong sense of property, and he said he would take steps to stop trespassers."

"He wouldn't shoot children, would he?" Emily asked anxiously.

"He was very upset," Papa warned. "I wouldn't risk

finding out." He turned to me. "As the oldest, you're responsible."

So what else was new? However, I said respectfully, "Yes, Papa."

"You weren't good children," Papa said.

It looked like we were going to lose Christmas. "We would have been early for school. . . ." Emily stopped when she saw Papa's face as he slowly realized the reason for the shortcut.

"But you were helping me," Papa said, finishing her sentence. He drummed his fingers guiltily against the counter.

"We were learning Chinese history too," Bobby said desperately.

Emily punched the air. "Death to the Manchus."

Despite himself, Papa had to laugh. It was always a good sign if you could get him to do that. "Well, it seemed like you did learn something. Since it was partly my fault, I guess the contest can continue. But only this once. If you're bad one more time, no Christmas."

Emily was so relieved that she risked teasing Papa. "I don't know if <u>you</u> should have Christmas, Papa."

Papa rubbed his head. "That is hardly a punishment. I don't want Christmas." Papa smiled like his old chipper self. "So what did you learn in school today?"

I always dreaded this moment when Papa quizzed us. I thought he ought to trust us to be diligent and not make us prove it. I resented it in a way, considering how much he depended upon me for other things.

Emily told him about some of the presidents she had learned about. One question always led to another with Papa, so the interrogation seemed endless.

"Who is this Tho-mas Jeff'son?"

"*Thomas Jefferson,*" I said, correcting his pronunciation.

He repeated it several times, though he never got close to the right way to say it. It was such a contrast to Mr. Barrington's clear, elegant enunciation. "Well, who is he?"

Then it was Bobby's turn. He informed Papa about the number of planets in our solar system. As I listened to each of them recite, I grew more and more resentful. If the school year covered about nine months and there were four weeks in a month and there were five days in a week, then it meant one hundred eighty days of recitation—less holidays, of course. That meant I had stood before him and recited my lessons around one thousand and eight hundred times. By the time I graduated from high school, it would be over two thousand times. Two thousand times!

I was so busy doing my calculations that I did not hear Papa at first. Since I was in high school, it took me longer to go through the day's lessons. "I asked, 'What about you, Joan?'"

I bet Mr. Barrington didn't cross-examine Victoria this way. "I learned lots of things, Papa," I said. "Why do you have to quiz me?"

Papa rocked back on his stool. "What a funny thing to say. I'm your father." It went without saying that he could do most anything because he was my father.

I wanted to tell Papa that my good grades ought to be

enough proof that I worked hard. I shouldn't have to go through a quiz every afternoon. But Emily poked me. "We have to keep Papa in a good mood," she whispered.

So I held back what I really wanted to say, but I couldn't resist getting in a dig. "In world history we learned all about Torquemada today. He made his living interrogating people." If he hadn't been a monk, he would have made a good father.

"Imagine that," Papa said.

I felt a little guilty about making fun of Papa, so I began reciting as customers came in. As Papa took care of them, he asked me questions.

When I was finished, I asked him, "Do you want some tea, Papa?"

He stared at the glass. "I haven't been feeling too well. Miss Lucy said that warm milk always settles her stomach." He patted his own for emphasis. "But I can't say that I fancy the taste of this."

I felt guilty for comparing him to Mr. Barrington, so I dabbed the milk mustache away with my mittened fingers. "Well, let me know if you need anything."

He dabbed at his mouth as well. "What would I do without you?"

"Go through life with a white mustache," I teased and then added, "Papa, can I go sledding?"

"Have you done your homework? Have you done your chores?" Papa demanded.

"No," I said in a small voice. No one else had to work as hard as we did. It just wasn't fair.

seven 

Speedy Bobby whipped through his homework, and I could hear the thump downstairs as he finished his chores. Emily rushed through her written homework almost as fast and then poked me. "Come on, Joan. We have to work on my pineapple."

If I hadn't been in a hurry myself, I would have helped her. But I still had hopes of joining the Barringtons sledding. "I've got work of my own."

"Be that way." Emily sniffed and went into the kitchen to start on her pineapple.

I should have reviewed Bobby's and Emily's homework too. However, by the time I finished my schoolwork, it had already grown dim outside my window. The sun would have set by the time I finished my chores. Today the laundry seemed like a prison, and I wanted to be free.

I stumped downstairs to the counter, where Papa

slumped on a stool with his arms wrapped around himself and his head swathed in his ragged cotton muffler. Mama was wearing almost as many layers as she kept him company, doing the ciphering in the ledger with her own system and her own notations.

From the drying room came the drip-drip of water from that day's washing. Mama and Papa looked as miserable in this weather as I felt.

"I'm ready for my chores, Papa," I said.

"Mmpf," he said.

Mama folded her arms. "You can go sledding. Just be back before dark."

"What about my chores?" I asked, puzzled.

"Your father did yours and Emily's," Mama said. "Don't get spoiled."

I should have felt grateful, but after all these years, I could only think it was about time.

I mean, even if I knew where to go, how did they expect me to walk there, sled with my friends, and still be back before dark? But I knew Mama would simply tell me not to go then. And I was determined to try to reach the party on the hill.

Sometimes I felt as if my parents kept me in a jar on a shelf. I could hear everyone else playing happily outside, but I couldn't even cry in frustration, because I would have drowned in my tears. I was determined that today was not going to be one of those times. There should be plenty of tracks from the others' sleds being dragged along. I would follow them to the hill.

"Thank you," I said, darting back into the laundry to bundle up.

As I stepped outside, Emily ran toward me. Miss Lucy was already there rolling up another ball of snow. *"Do you want to build a snow sheriff? He's going to catch any bullies and put them in jail forever,"* Emily said.

"What about the pineapple?" I asked in a whisper.

I noticed a spot of flour on her cheek from making papier-mâché. "Done," Emily said, and eyed me indignantly. "You're starting to sound like Mama."

Before I had a chance to mull over that scary thought, I heard an automobile honk its horn. The sound carried through the clear, still winter air, and I looked over to see Mr. Barrington and Victoria barreling down the snowy street.

I almost broke down and cried. They had already finished and had come back to move. I had missed all the fun yet again, thanks to my spoilsport father.

"Hullo," Victoria called with a wave. *"We left Ann and the others to come back and see if you had changed your mind about going with us."*

"The sledding's glorious," Mr. Barrington chimed in. *"All that was wanting was your company."*

Miss Lucy dusted the snow from her mittens. *"Don't you want to pick up your keys first?"*

"Later. The slopes await us." He got out of the car. *"Miss Lucy, would you like to come sledding with us? The snow is deep and powdery and the air is brisk."*

"And me," Emily chimed in, thrusting herself against my hip.

"And you," Mr. Barrington agreed, grinning down at her.

Miss Lucy was a bit flustered. *"Let me get my hat."*

"Allow me." With a gallant flourish, Mr. Barrington presented her with his hat.

Though it engulfed Miss Lucy's head, she laughed like a young girl herself. *"Done,"* she said, adjusting the brim so she could see.

Opening the gate in the fence, Mr. Barrington ushered us through. *"Ladies, your humble chariot awaits."*

I felt grand as a queen as we climbed into that great machine. I counted this as my first real journey in an automobile—you could hardly count the morning's trip since that had lasted only seconds.

Once we were seated, he cried out, *"Tallyho!"* and, turning the car away from the curb, made a U-turn in the street, tires grunting through the slush.

I thought I saw the laundry's front door open. Papa's muffler-swathed head poked out into the cold while the motor roared into life. I waved to him and then clung excitedly to the car door. And I couldn't help thinking that if Papa were like Mr. Barrington, my life would not only be easier but much more fun.

As the needle swung higher and higher on the speedometer, the wind whipped through the open windows and the world raced by. Stores and houses flashed past like the sets in a movie, and I found myself gripping the dashboard and bracing my feet against the floor.

When Mr. Barrington saw I was nervous, he only laughed and went faster. On the way to the hill, he carried on a conversation with Miss Lucy, yelling his questions to her and straining to hear her shouted answers.

He seemed amused when Miss Lucy pointed out his grandfather's bank. *"So that old pile was Grandfather's?"* he asked. *"It looks like a dungeon."*

A few blocks away the houses gave way to tall trees with bare branches that reached outward in a wiry tangle. Around their trunks the vines were also brown and bare of leaves, so the trees seemed to be wearing shaggy coats. They stood like frozen sentries on the rolling white landscape.

After a quarter mile we neared a white mound fringed by trees. There were black dots racing down its sides, and as we got closer I could hear the shrill voices of children.

Mr. Barrington helped Miss Lucy from the car. Her face was all red and she was out of breath, but she was chipper as a lark. *"I haven't had that much fun since the Flood. Thank you so much, Mr. Barrington."*

Mr. Barrington's teeth flashed. *"James."*

Miss Lucy beamed. *"Well, thank you, James."*

"The excitement is just beginning, ladies," he said, putting a hand to her elbow for support.

It was obvious that he didn't know Miss Lucy at all, because she shook him off. *"I'm not going to break, James,"* she insisted. *"My great-aunt was shinnying up trees at the age of ninety. She collected birds' eggs. Blowing out the yolks made her a bit light-headed, though. But she wound up with lungs like a blacksmith's bellows."*

"She must have been useful when you flew kites," Mr. Barrington teased.

Miss Lucy walked through the snow proudly. *"She never went in for anything as frivolous as that."* She pointed at a spot of red. *"Look, that staghorn sumac's sprouted early."*

Suddenly Miss Lucy was like a toddler who had stumbled into a room full of toys. She moved ahead of us excitedly, pointing at one thing and another. I guess it had been a while since she had been out of town. Finally she halted before a tree where there was a cluster of fruit like bright-red bubbles. *"In the mornings you might see cardinals around here."*

Mr. Barrington leaned his head to the side as he listened to the delighted, high-pitched screams. *"But for now I think it's a bit too noisy."*

We made our way to the foot of the hill. Several girls sat on sleds gliding down toward us, runners hissing through the snow.

"There's Janey," Emily said, and she ran toward her friend, madly waving her hand.

Stomach on the boards, a boy zigzagged recklessly down the slopes past one girl after another. I recognized Bobby's whoop. *"Out of the way!"* he called. His voice grew louder as he neared us.

We jumped out of the way barely in time.

Bobby skimmed away from us as smoothly as a bug skittering over a pond.

"Now that's how to sled." Mr. Barrington laughed as he flicked off the snow my brother had sprayed over us in his wake.

Deciding that I'd make him pay later, I began to brush off Miss Lucy. As we were cleaning ourselves, Ann floated toward us serenely. She sat upright upon her red wooden sled with her hands folded primly over her lap so that her skirts couldn't go flying up. It was a great contrast to the way my brother had cannonballed down the hill.

"*You made it,*" she said. The sled was moving so slowly that it was easy for her to hop off and get to her feet.

"*Allow me,*" Mr. Barrington said, and stooped to take the sled ropes. Ann made a point of ignoring me as we climbed the hill. She chattered away at Victoria. "*I suppose this can't compare with the Alps, but we do what we can.*" And on and on she went.

Mr. Barrington good-naturedly kept pace next to them while I brought up the rear with Miss Lucy. Now that he wasn't watching, she had taken my arm for support.

She squinted slightly as she studied his back. "*James is such a lively fellow, don't you think?*"

I squeezed her hand. "*He needs you to keep him in line.*"

There were about fifty girls of various ages, sledding down the slope or climbing back up or waiting on top for their turn. There were about as many boys, who threw themselves belly down on their sleds with loud yells and plunged through the snow in huge sheets of snowy spray.

Havana greeted me at the top as she maneuvered a bright-blue sled toward the edge. "*I didn't think you were coming,*" she said, and smiled at Miss Lucy. "*And Miss Bradshaw. How did Joan pry you from your piano?*" Like half the town, Havana had taken music lessons from Miss Lucy.

Miss Lucy released me quickly. "*I thought I'd show you young folks a thing or two. May I?*" she asked, gesturing toward the sled, which had huge bouquets of flowers painted on its surface.

Havana stepped away from her sled but looked at Miss Lucy doubtfully. *"Are you sure?"*

"Quite sure," Miss Lucy insisted, and briskly stretched a leg over the sled and sat down.

Victoria had Ann's red sled. She was about to fling herself down on her stomach like a boy. *"Let's show those boys some real sledding, Miss Bradshaw."*

"Victoria!" Ann said, scandalized. *"You'd have to lie down on the sled, and you know what happens next."* She lowered her lids discreetly.

Most of the time Victoria seemed like such a young lady; but she had this impish streak too, which I had seen before on the basketball court. *"But you go so much faster when you're on your stomach."* Victoria shrugged. *"Which is just what I would like."*

Ann motioned toward her skirt. *"But then this would go flying up and everyone could see your . . . you know?"*

"My petticoat?" Victoria said, deliberately using an ancient word. She seemed vaguely amused.

Mr. Barrington arched an eyebrow. *"When in Rome, dear."*

With a sigh Victoria sat upright, gripping the sides of the sled. She barely had time to smile at Miss Lucy before Ann and Mr. Barrington had leaned forward and pushed her. She went down the slope sitting upon the sled as stiffly as a doll, bobbing up and down as the runners followed every rise and dip on the slope. Next to her Miss Lucy kept the same sedate pace.

Mr. Barrington winked at me. *"Not much of a challenge, is it?"*

The boys were a real menace as they shot like rockets

around Victoria and Miss Lucy.

It had been the same in Ohio. *"Girls can't go down the hill lying down,"* I said.

"Pity," he murmured.

Nonetheless, when Victoria brought both sleds back up, handing one to him and one to me, he sat up on his.

"You're a boy," I said. *"You can go down on your stomach."*

"But I am far too advanced in years to be considered a boy," he said. *"And so we tribal elders must respect our dignity. Gravitas. Gravitas."*

I knew better, though. He was a real gentleman determined to keep me company. Havana gave me a shove, while Victoria and Ann did the honors for Mr. Barrington.

I loved that first second when I plunged down the hill. For a moment the world was silvery and misty, and the sun was as pale as buttermilk. And the next instant the whole world seemed to tilt when the sled did; and then there was nothing but the sound of the runners and my own screams.

I glanced at Mr. Barrington to see how he was enjoying it and caught him stifling a yawn. I suppose it must have been a bit tame compared to what he must have been used to. He looked sheepish when he caught me staring at him.

Miss Lucy was clapping her hands at the bottom of the hill in encouragement. With her was Emily. Her clothes were already mussed up from playing in the snow, and her hair was matted to her sweaty forehead. I'd have to straighten her up before we got home or Mama would make her pay for her fun. Daughters of a scholar couldn't look like raggedy beggars.

When I asked Miss Lucy if she was coming back up with us, she shook her head. *"Someone should be ready to set broken bones. I made my point."*

To be honest, she looked a bit cold, as if she should have dressed warmer than just a coat. In fact, by the third time I had gone down the hill, she had gone to sit in the car.

I began to worry about her so when we had slid down the hill once again, I asked Mr. Barrington if he thought Miss Lucy was comfortable.

Mr. Barrington smiled affectionately in her direction. *"That lady would rather turn into an icicle than admit she's cold."* He began to unbutton his own coat. *"So I'll make sure she takes mine."*

"But you'll freeze then," I said.

"Not if I stay in the car. Someone should keep her company anyway," he said.

As I watched him stalk through the snow toward his automobile, I couldn't help thinking that there really were gentlemen. They weren't just imaginary creations of Henrietta's romances.

Emily and Janey went back up with me, towing Janey's sled parallel to mine. When I found Victoria up there, I explained that her father was staying with Miss Lucy in the car.

Victoria had the same smile as her father. *"Shall we see how fast we can get down to him? Let's sled like the boys."*

"But you can't," Ann protested.

"I don't see any sign on it that says we can't," Victoria teased.

My friend Henrietta looked at Victoria disapprovingly. She liked to sample wild adventures in her reading rather than in real life.

Havana, though, was tempted. *"Well . . ."*

"Havana," Henrietta said, and grabbed her arm, holding on to her for dear life.

Beneath the princess mask Victoria wore most of the time, there was a strange wildness I kept glimpsing. Perhaps it was her different upbringing.

Victoria held out her hands. *"Well, would you mind if I borrowed your sled?"*

Ann gave a little gasp. *"You're really going to do that?"*

"I'd like a more exhilarating ride." Victoria's eyes darted around the circle of faces, but there was no girl who would take up the dare. Especially Ann.

"What will your father say?" Ann asked, shocked.

I couldn't help thinking of Papa's reaction if he caught me doing that.

Victoria picked up the sled and hugged it against her. *"Why should he be upset?"* she asked, with such self-assurance that I envied her. If I had a father like hers, I might have the confidence to dare anything.

The boys and girls around us began whispering and pointing, but Victoria took a step toward me excitedly, as if I were her fellow conspirator. *"Let's show those old fuddy-duddies and try a real challenge. How about it, Joan?"*

I knew what I should say, and I knew what my parents would want me to say; but her excitement was infectious. I liked the feeling that there were just the two of us willing to take on the world. Just once in my life I wanted to be a little wild too.

My mouth had a life of its own. "*Let's,*" I said, feeling almost as daring as Victoria.

My reward was a secret, conspiratorial smile. "*I knew you would.*" And she raced toward the edge with the sled in her hands. "*Come on, Joan,*" she called.

And the next moment she had launched herself and her sled into the air.

They both bounced when they landed in the snow, but she came down on top of the sled. It was a perfect belly flop. Then she began flashing down the slope.

It reassured me to see that only the hem of her skirt rose, rippling slightly.

She could be as wild as her hairdo. Bits of snow were scattered over her flushed cheeks.

Stooping, I picked up Havana's sled and raced toward the slope.

I knew that if I stopped to think, I would talk myself out of it—and lose what goodwill I had earned with Victoria. And the closer to the edge I got, the steeper the hill seemed.

"*Joanie,*" I heard Emily say in horror. It was obvious from the way I carried the sled what I was going to do.

"*Come back here,*" Bobby yelled angrily. As he ran toward me, a sled bounced up and down over the snow on the tow rope.

"*Bet you a dessert that I beat you,*" I shouted defiantly.

And with a kick of my legs I flew through the air. I'd had time to study the boys' technique by now. Unfortunately, I lacked Victoria's coordination. I nearly lost my grip on the sled when my stomach slammed against its boards. Somehow, though, I managed to hang on to it.

I heard Bobby shout again as I began whizzing down the slope. It was his turn now to eat my spray.

Snow plumed upward on either side like thin, large wings, and the trees seemed to tumble past like falling dominos.

This was so much better! I had been a snail before. I gripped the sled front till my knuckles went numb as I sped after Victoria. All I could see of her was the soles of her boots amid the shower of snow. And my skirt felt as flat as hers. People had been making far too much of an issue about girls belly flopping. This was much better than bumping along sedately.

Though I had a head start, Bobby glided up on his borrowed sled so that we were side by side for a moment. *"Are you crazy?"*

However, I'd also studied the slope by now and picked out the smoothest, most even part. I lay low against the sled boards, pressing my cheek against the wood and steering the runners. Bobby's mouth dropped open as I pulled away.

I had never gone this fast. Victoria was right. This was fun. I picked up more speed the farther I went. I could not see Victoria, only the spray of snow in front of me; but through the hiss of the runners I thought I could hear Victoria's giddy, carefree laughter floating up toward me.

From the hilltop and along the sides, the boys were

begging Bobby to catch me. However, I was too far ahead. And the girls were urging me just as loudly to beat him. At the bottom of the hill was Mr. Barrington's car. I could see the steam rising from his and Miss Lucy's breath.

Suddenly I felt my dress lift up. I glanced behind me and saw the blue cloth rising like a sail. The cheering and shouting stopped abruptly.

For some reason, my slip still clung to my legs, but it was bad enough for the boys to see that. Frantically, I reached one hand behind me to pull my dress back down.

However, that not only distracted me from steering but also changed my balance on the sled. And at that speed I could not hold on with just one hand.

The sled came to life underneath me and seemed to leap up. Thinking about the sharp runners, I tried to push myself away. I heard the sled tumble through the snow, and then I was falling after it.

Blue sky and white snow took turns speeding past; and I didn't see how I could ever stop—unless I slammed into a tree or a rock. I heard the sled bang against something. When I finally hit a snowbank, my first thought was to be relieved. But everything seemed so white around me, and I realized the force of my fall had plunged me deep into it.

eight 

From somewhere far away, Emily was calling my name. *"Joan, Joan, are you all right?"*

Other voices asked the same urgent question, but they seemed to float down to me as if I were within a deep well.

I tried to answer but only got a mouthful of snow. And for a moment, I panicked, feeling icy water clutching at me.

Then someone was tugging at my ankles. *"Can you move?"* I thought it was Miss Lucy's voice.

I kicked my legs and felt hands on my shoulders.

"Joan, Joan, are you all right?" Victoria's voice seemed to be by my ear.

"You're going to be all right," Miss Lucy said. Her voice seemed to be by my other ear.

I tried to answer but got more snow. Continuing to panic, I tried to wriggle out of the snowbank. In no time, though, the snow seemed to lift from above me. When I opened my eyes, I saw a ring of faces above me. I realized I was at the bottom of the hill and had mistaken the snow beneath me for the cold water of a well.

Mr. Barrington himself lifted me out, and I saw a dozen others who had helped to dig away the snow.

Bobby came up towing Havana's sled behind him. "*Everything's fine. The sled isn't damaged.*"

"*I'm glad.*" I sat up slowly, but the world kept spinning around. "*Because I may be. I feel dizzy.*"

Emily flopped on her knees beside my head, and her face loomed over me. "*But you're the fastest.*" Her hands were on my shoulders, and her breath rose from her mouth in wisps of steam.

I saw one stubborn brown leaf that had somehow managed to cling to a snow-laden branch over her head.

Miss Lucy's anxious face appeared over me, hiding the tree. "*Let her breathe, Emily.*" Victoria tugged Emily away as Miss Lucy knelt beside me. "*Can you move your arms and legs, Joan?*" she asked again.

Anxiously, I moved first one limb and then another. "*Yes.*"

I shrank inside when I saw Mr. Barrington kneel on my other side. I expected him to scold me like Papa would have done about being reckless.

However, Mr. Barrington didn't even blink. "*No pain in your sides? No trouble breathing?*" he asked solicitously.

I took several experimental breaths. "*No, sir.*" When I tried to sit up, though, I still felt a little dizzy—almost as if I were not quite in my body. I mean my body might have been sitting in the snow, but I felt as if whatever was me was floating somewhere above it. For a moment I wondered if Papa had been right and my dream soul had really slipped free.

"Help her up, James," Miss Lucy said.

Mr. Barrington obligingly put his strong arms around me to give me support; and suddenly I felt like I had slipped back inside my body again. *"I think we should take you to a doctor,"* he suggested.

Doctors, though, would mean my parents would find out; and that could mean the end of all winter outings. And there was the Christmas contest. *"No, no doctors,"* I said frantically.

"At the very least I think we should take you home," Mr. Barrington said. *"Can you get into my car?"*

"She'll need a nurse," Emily said instantly, eager to ride in the car.

Bobby horned in too. *"I'm her next of kin."*

Emily had found my hat and jammed it forcefully down over my head. *"We share the same bed, so I'm next to her every night. That makes me even more nexter."*

Bobby was not about to surrender the chance of riding in the car. *"But I'm older than you, so that makes me nearer kin than you are."*

"Yes, I think you should both accompany your sister," Mr. Barrington said kindly. He helped lift me to my feet. *"Victoria, will you stay with our guests? I'll come back for all of you."*

Victoria was busy brushing the snow from her clothes and trying to tame her hair. *"Of course,"* she said calmly.

Victoria was such a bundle of contradictions. She could be a wild girl, scandalizing everyone. And yet other times she seemed as old as her father. She not only spoke with more maturity than us but acted that way too. Perhaps it was because her father treated her like a companion rather than the disappointment I seemed to be to my parents.

Miss Lucy got on one side and Mr. Barrington got on the other as they helped me toward his car. When I passed Ann, she glared at me from the crowd. But I was still a little too woozy to feel any triumph. However, as I started to get into the car, I noticed the scratches and dent. *"Oh, no, your lovely car. Did I do that?"*

From behind me Bobby commented in Chinese so the others wouldn't understand. "The sled did. If it had been your head that had hit the car, its side would have been caved in."

In distress I stared at the damage. *"We'll pay for it, of course."* I just hoped the cost of repairs wasn't too high. Even though we were finally making a profit on the laundry, I knew that we did not have much money in reserve.

And there was the Christmas contest. "I just lost our Christmas," I said to Emily. "I'm sorry."

Emily scrunched up her face in a scowl, but Mr. Barrington patted me on the shoulder before she could speak. *"Nonsense, my dear. It was stupid of me to park it where I did. I'm just lucky you didn't get hurt. Dents can always be fixed."*

Though I was relieved to hear him say that, I felt

obligated to make a second offer. *"You're sure?"*

"Don't give it another thought." Mr. Barrington helped me into the backseat. He was so different from Papa.

"Please don't mention this to our parents," Emily begged.

"But Joan could be hurt," Miss Lucy said.

"They're worried about Christmas," Mr. Barrington said to her with a twinkle in his eye and looked down at Emily. *"Afraid Santa Claus won't bring you anything?"*

"It's something like that," I said quickly.

"Then we'll forget it ever happened," Mr. Barrington assured me and glanced at Miss Lucy. *"Right, Miss Lucy?"*

She hesitated, but she couldn't resist Mr. Barrington's charm either. *"Well, I suppose so."*

"Thank you," I said fervently. Mr. Barrington was so incredibly generous.

While Miss Lucy climbed up beside me, Emily ran around to the passenger side of the front seat and clambered in before Bobby could.

She twisted around in triumph as Bobby had to climb up beside Miss Lucy.

In the meantime Mr. Barrington produced a blanket from the trunk.

He opened it with a flourish. *"Voilà! We don't want your knees getting cold."* Tenderly he spread the blanket over us.

"Good-bye! Good-bye!" Emily was already waving farewell to everyone and anything in sight.

Mr. Barrington jumped into the front seat and entered

into Emily's game. *"Where to, m'lady?"*

Emily tilted her nose in the air as we had seen the ritzy ladies do in the movies. *"Home, James."*

Aghast, I glared at her. *"He's not your chauffeur."*

However, Mr. Barrington good-naturedly touched the brim of his hat. *"Home it is, m'lady."*

Emily made a face at me and then began waving farewell again, using both hands this time. *"Good-bye! Good-bye!"*

When we reached the edge of town, Emily sat up straight without my having to tell her. Heads swiveled to stare at the fancy car as it purred past. After he had pulled up to the curb by the laundry, Mr. Barrington put on the brake and put the car into neutral. Turning around, he smiled at me. *"You really must come to tea sometime, Joan. I can see you'll be a very good influence on my Victoria."*

I could barely contain my excitement at the thought. Tea with them would be as splendid as anything in a book. *"Yes, sir. Thank you, sir."* I paused before sliding after Bobby and Miss Lucy out the door. *"Are you sure we can't pay for the damages?"*

This time he did not even deign to answer aloud. He pursed his lips together and shook his head as if it were beneath us to discuss money.

As she opened her door, Emily grabbed one last feel of the leather upholstery. *"'Bye, and thanks. One day I'm going to have a car twice as big."*

Mr. Barrington laughed. *"I trust you'll give me a ride."*

"You can count on it," Emily said, and squealed in

indignation when I grabbed her by the waist and hauled her to the sidewalk. If she'd had her way, she would have sat in the car till doomsday chatting with Mr. Barrington. I couldn't really blame her.

"Good-bye, Mr. Barrington." Bobby slammed the door shut.

"I'll arrange to deliver our things tonight," Mr. Barrington said to Miss Lucy.

"Let me get you the keys," Miss Lucy said, starting toward her house.

"No time. The Barrington Express has more pickups to make." With one last cheery wave, Mr. Barrington put the car into gear and swung it around.

As he headed back for the hill, I heard Mama say, "That's a very fancy car."

She was standing on the top step. "When I heard the noisy thing, I looked out the window and saw you getting out of it." She was waiting for an explanation.

My arms were still around Emily's waist. I tried to appear casual as I shifted them to her shoulders, where my forearms could keep a light pressure on her throat. "We were sledding, and Mr. Barrington kindly gave us a lift home."

"Your faces are all red and your clothes are wet." Mama came down and felt Emily's and Bobby's wrists for a feverish pulse. "If you die of pneumonia, don't blame me."

Bobby was still staring after the car. "He must have some horsepower under that hood. I bet he could get up a hill like that." He snapped his fingers.

"The hill will still be there whether you race or walk." Mama began to shepherd Emily and me inside.

As Emily trudged past, she said excitedly, "Mr. Barrington's been to England, Mama."

However, Mama was unimpressed. "And your father and I come from China."

"But he's been on top of the Eiffel Tower." Emily would have slipped on a snow-covered patch, but I caught her.

"And your father's been on top of the Great Wall." Mama pointed at a shovel resting against the side of the stairs. "Bobby, shovel the walk."

"But I'm cold, Mama," Bobby protested.

"You should have thought of that before you went out to play in the snow for two hours." She gave him a shove toward the shovel. "Shoveling will warm you up."

Still Bobby tried to weasel out of the chore. "But it's dark."

Mama, though, was relentless. "There's enough light from the streetlamp."

I had been trying to avoid Mama's eagle-eyed scrutiny; but when she touched my arm, she drew back. "Joan, you're soaked all the way through."

"The snow was flying," I said, and sneezed. "Ah-choo."

Mama frowned as she shoved Emily and me inside. "And so are the colds."

The warmth from the laundry swept all around us as soon as we entered the door.

Papa came out from the washroom when he heard the bell. "I thought it might be a customer desperate for his drawers."

He must have just finished washing a batch of clothes,

because the front of his shirt was wet and his sleeves were still rolled up. His hands and arms were still a lobster red from being immersed in hot water.

In Miss Blake's office that morning I had seen Mr. Barrington's hands. They had been smooth and white, a gentleman's hands. For a moment I felt ashamed of Papa—and right away I told myself I was being awful. It was those red, rough hands that put clothes on my back and food on the table.

Papa took in my rumpled clothes and idly brushed some snow that still clung to my shoulders. "Did you have an accident?" he asked, worried.

"If you catch a cold, it's your own fault," Mama grunted.

I had never deliberately hidden the truth from my parents—well, not on big things. However, I couldn't help contrasting their attitudes with Mr. Barrington's. He made Victoria feel like a princess riding in a fancy automobile, being waited upon by a father who doted on her. My whole soul yearned to be her.

In contrast, if my parents weren't criticizing my behavior, then it was my study habits—or my posture, or the shine of my shoes. Everything I did reflected upon the family—and usually everything I did was wrong. None of my friends had to go under a microscope to be inspected for flaws.

If they hadn't had such strange attitudes or forced us into this awful contest, I would have told them everything that had happened. They were practically asking to be lied to.

"We were just sledding," I said. I glanced at Emily in warning. She was keeping her lips shut tight. She wanted Christmas as much as I did. I knew I could trust Bobby to keep his mouth shut.

To Papa, sledding was just another odd quirk of American life. "It's very messy. You should change," he said anxiously. Then, with a wince, he put a hand to his stomach.

"Is something wrong?" Mama asked solicitously.

"My stomach's bothering me a little," he said as he rubbed it. "I think I'll skip dinner."

"I'll warm up some more milk for you," Mama said to him. "Joan, watch the front."

With a sigh of relief I leaned against the counter. "We got away with it," I said to Emily and Bobby. I realized how selfish I was sounding. "I'm sorry about Papa's stomachache though."

Still, it couldn't have come at a better time.

nine

The Barringtons moved in that night with a good deal of rumbling and a good deal of music. They set up a phonograph as soon as they could. Funny, but there weren't any moving men. I guess they hadn't wanted to work that late. I hoped I hadn't delayed them.

The noise annoyed Mama. She kept glaring out the kitchen window. "How is your papa ever going to sleep with such a racket?"

"How is Papa feeling?" I asked.

"His stomach's bothering him. I keep giving him milk to settle it, but it just doesn't seem to work." Mama sighed. A thump outside made her stare again. "If they're so rich, why are they moving themselves? Movers would do this only in respectable hours."

I thought I was really worldly compared to Mama. "They probably have a lot of delicate things they bought all over the world. If I had things like that, I'd want just me to handle them."

Mama arched an eyebrow. "Oh, you would, would you? Then it's better to save your money and buy practical things that can't break."

Practical was another word for cheap and ugly. All my life I had been surrounded by sensible things. I ached to just once have something that was fine and fragile and lovely.

Even so, the moving noise made it hard to get to sleep; and when I finally did, I dreamed I was a giant pineapple lying in a bakery on a wooden table, and Emily and Bobby were trying to squeeze me under a giant rolling pin.

"Joanie, Joanie," Emily was saying urgently.

I tried to push her away. "Stop it. I don't want to be flat."

But she seized my outthrust arm and pinched my wrist viciously. "Wake up. It's morning."

"Ow! Stop that." I sat up groggily. It took me a moment to realize that I was not in a bakery but still in our bedroom in the laundry.

The next instant I had an armful of anxious Emily. "Hurry, Joanie," she urged as she slid off the bed again. "We don't want to be late today."

The last few words came muffled through Emily's dress. Since she had neglected to unbutton the back, it stuck around her head and just a few wisps of hair showed through the open collar. Nonetheless, she kept tugging so much that I was afraid she'd tear it.

It was hard to set her to rights, because she kept hopping up and down impatiently, afraid of being late and risking a presentless Christmas. I knew a bit more about the family's finances. Though the laundry was turning a small profit now, we still had a lot of expenses. I didn't know if Emily was going to get that doll she wanted. Still, I didn't want to make her even more anxious and excited, so I held my peace.

When I had repaired what damage I could, Emily bolted from the room.

Papa was in the kitchen, but he was only drinking milk again, as if his stomach bothered him. Even the simple rice gruel with slices of hundred-day-old eggs was too much for him.

Emily slurped hers down so noisily, Mama frowned. "Mind your manners."

Emily wiped her mouth on her sleeve. "I don't want to be late."

Though Bobby and I ate a bit more slowly, we finished our meal quickly enough. Then, snatching up our lunches and schoolbooks, we tumbled outside into the rear courtyard formed by our laundry, Miss Lucy's house and the cottage. Miss Lucy's vegetable garden lay under the snow.

I paused for a moment to look at the fairy light in Miss Lucy's kitchen. Though it was the daytime, she had lit the candle. In today's brighter light, it seemed like the heart of a distant star. It seemed to wink at me. Things would be all right.

"Wait up," Emily said. Her books, bound by a strap, rested on both hands. And on top of the pile of books was her lunch, along with a gaudy pineapple about the size of Emily's head.

"Why are you carrying your pineapple that way?" I asked. "It could fall off." Indeed, it was already starting to tilt off the books.

"It's wet," Emily said.

Too late. I had already shoved it back. I saw the green stain on my mittens.

"Hey," Emily said. I had used too much force, and the pineapple's top had come to rest against her chin. By tilting the books and using her chin, Emily managed to shift the pineapple back to the center of the book stack away from her lunch. There were orange spots on the paper bag from where the pineapple had pressed against it. As she began to blow on it, I could see the green stain on her chin.

Bobby circled Emily and the pineapple with a critical eye. "Are pineapples supposed to be that color?"

In the sunlight the pineapple was a ghastly shade of orange. "It didn't look so bright last night in the kitchen light," I said.

Emily felt honor bound to defend her creation. "I think it's pretty."

Bobby leaned to one side and shut one eye as he studied the pineapple. "You would. It looks like you with green hair."

"You take that back!" As Emily started toward Bobby, the pineapple began to bobble dangerously.

"Watch it," I said, grabbing Emily's shoulder.

As a furious Emily stood rooted to one spot, Bobby began to dance around her. "It's got your pimples."

Emily did her best to pivot and yet keep her pineapple upright. "My skin is clear. You're the one with pimples."

Across the way Miss Lucy opened her door and peered out. *"I thought I heard you children."*

Bobby couldn't resist irritating Emily even more. *"Can you guess what that is, Miss Lucy?"* he asked, pointing.

Miss Lucy hesitated, staring at Emily's pineapple. *"Oh . . . uh . . ."*

"Certainly Miss Lucy knows," Emily maintained stoutly. *"Tell him Miss Lucy."*

"Yes, please do," Bobby urged.

"Oh . . . uh . . ."

From behind Emily I tried to pantomime a hula, but Bobby immediately cried, *"No fair."*

Rather timidly, Miss Lucy ventured, *"Kaiser Wilhelm?"*

As Bobby's laughter rang around the little courtyard, Miss Lucy tried to repair the damage as best she could. *"My eyes are getting old. What is it, Emily?"*

If you had asked her to name some biblical plagues at that moment, Emily would have mentioned frogs, locusts and brothers. *"A pineapple,"* she said, pouting.

Miss Lucy bent over to view it better. *"Well, yes. So it is. And a mighty handsome one it is too. It must be 'products of the states and territories' time."*

I nudged Emily to remind her of her manners. *"Thank you,"* she muttered.

Miss Lucy clasped her hands behind her back. *"Now you must come inside with me."*

"We really should be heading toward school," I said dutifully.

She glanced at the watch that hung on a chain around her neck. It had a little porcelain back with pink roses painted on it. *"Fiddlesticks. There's plenty of time. I wanted to show you what I found for our Christmas celebration."* She bounced up and down on the balls of her feet.

Though Emily was the youngest and Miss Lucy was the oldest there, they were the closest in temperament. *"You must like to give Christmas parties,"* Emily said enthusiastically.

Miss Lucy leaned her head to the side and stared absently off into the distance. *"Oh, heavens, we used to have big shindigs. But it seemed silly once there was only me."*

I could hear the loneliness in her voice. *"What a shame,"* I said sympathetically.

Emily could hear it too. *"What did you most like about your parties?"*

Miss Lucy bit her lip. *"There were lots of things—the music, the food, the tree."*

I longed to see it. *"You must have a lovely tree."*

"I haven't bothered until this year," Miss Lucy explained. *"But I will now. It took me all night to find the decorations in the attic. It's been a long time since I used them."*

Emily tottered past me with her pineapple. *"Ooo, let's see."*

"*Emily*," I said in frustration.

Eyes on her pineapple, she plowed on like a determined little locomotive. *"Miss Lucy asked us in."*

I was going to remind her about being late, but then I saw the expression on Miss Lucy's face. She looked as eager as a child at her first real birthday party. Emily knew the risk just as well as I did. She was doing this for her friend. "Come on, Bobby," I said.

When we had taken off our coats and galoshes, we followed Miss Lucy into her parlor, where I saw that she was quite literally ankle deep in Christmas. Dusty boxes covered every surface.

She nodded toward the floor, which was covered with boxes. *"It's been so long since I used them that I forgot where they were."*

Emily gave a little sneeze when she lifted the lid of the nearest box. She sucked in her breath. *"How pretty."* She held up the lid for Bobby and me to see. Inside was an ornate angel of gilt and porcelain.

Pleased, Miss Lucy stood behind her. *"It was my grandmother's."*

Each box held a new marvel: delicate, shiny glass ornaments from Germany, a manger set from Italy, Venetian candleholders. Some of them were her grandmother's, some of them her mother's or her aunt's.

The best were the handblown ornaments. *"These are spheres from Germany. My, it's like seeing old friends again,"* Miss Lucy said. She held up a delicate, shiny glass globe.

"If I had things this pretty, I'd have them out every year," Emily said.

"I should have . . . but . . . somehow it's not the same

without friends and loved ones around," Miss Lucy said wistfully.

She sounded terribly lonely. *"But you have friends and family."*

She pursed her lips. *"I know plenty of people, but I made the mistake of outlasting all my close friends and immediate family."*

Neither Bobby nor I knew what to say. Emily did, though. *"But you have us."*

It wasn't like Miss Lucy to mope around for very long. She gave her shoulders a little shake. *"That's right. Because of all of you, I'm going to have a wonderful Christmas again."*

Finally I understood why she had pushed Papa so hard about celebrating Christmas.

"What's in here?" Emily asked as she started to reach for another box.

"Maybe you'd better let me and Joan handle them," Bobby said to Emily as she reached for a box. *"They're all pretty old."*

As at any suggestion from Bobby, Emily started to bristle. *"I'll be careful."*

For once, I had to agree with Bobby. *"But they're full of memories. That makes them irreplaceable."*

"Emily will be careful," Miss Lucy said, and gestured.

Tilting her head back, Emily lifted her nose imperiously and then picked up the box and set it on the floor. Inside were more spheres, which she treated as if they would disappear when she touched them.

While we inspected the contents of each box, Miss Lucy gazed into the distance. *"You should have seen our house at Christmas. It was always bursting with people. My grandfather was famous for his hospitality. We always had such a big tree, and it would be all ablaze with light. People used to say he really had the spirit of Christmas."*

I understood more and more why she was so eager to get out all her grandfather's old things again. It had to be sad to live in a dark house that had once been so alive at Christmas and to celebrate it only with ghosts. And I decided to make this the best Christmas for everyone.

In the meantime Emily's eyes widened as she tried to calculate. *"He must have gotten a lot of presents."*

Miss Lucy laughed at the notion. *"If my grandfather had worried about acquiring things, he would never have become a country doctor in the first place. His patients were his guests, and none of them had very much at any time of the year, let alone Christmas."* She hunched forward eagerly. *"But what do you children want for Christmas?"*

"A doll," Emily piped up without hesitation.

"A sled," Bobby said.

We'd barely avoided losing Christmas yesterday. I wasn't going to count on any presents. *"Nothing,"* I said.

Miss Lucy wagged a finger at me. *"I've seen you looking at the fairy light. Wouldn't you like one for yourself?"*

"*They're too expensive*," I said, and tried to change the subject. *"But what would you like?"*

Miss Lucy clasped her hands in her lap. *"You children."* She glanced at the boxes. *"Oh, it's going to be as much fun as in grandfather's day."*

We began having so much fun planning our own Christmas party that we lost track of time.

When we had gone through most of the boxes, there came a knock at the door. *"Miss Lucy,"* Papa said, *"my clock stop. What time is it?"*

"Let me see," Miss Lucy said.

Miss Lucy looked at her watch again, but this time her thumb flicked open the top. I always loved that first moment when the chimes began to play "Silver Threads Among the Gold." As the first notes began, she brought the watch to within a few inches of her eyes. Before the tune could finish playing she clicked it shut in alarm. *"Goodness. I lost track of the time. You children are going to be late."*

"Good-bye," I said, grabbing handfuls of coats and galoshes. As we got dressed hastily, Miss Lucy opened the door and told Papa the time.

"Thank you," he said politely, but he didn't seem in much of a hurry to go back home and set his clock. I stood for a moment on one foot as I tried to pull the galosh over my other. Stricken, I looked up at Papa.

"Hello, Papa."

If it had been Mama who had caught us, we would have had a five-minute lecture. Papa, though, seemed more resigned than angry. *"Better go school,"* he said. Thanking Miss Lucy again, he turned around and went back into the laundry.

I think the clock had been an excuse to remind us of the time. It was like Papa to use gentle methods to keep us out of trouble. And that made me feel even worse for failing him.

Bidding Miss Lucy a hasty good-bye, we tumbled outside into the courtyard.

"We're going to have to take that shortcut again," Bobby whispered grimly.

I was feeling reckless. It seemed no matter what I did, I got in trouble. "I guess so."

Emily steadied the pineapple with her chin, which was still green. "I don't want to go across the pasture," she protested. "Farmer Pynchon warned us."

"You want Christmas, don't you?" I asked.

"Ye-e-s," Emily admitted reluctantly.

"If we're late to school, Mama and Papa might use that as an excuse. And then you can kiss Christmas goodbye."

Clutching the damp pineapple, Emily shut her eyes and sighed like a tragic nickelodeon star. "If we must."

ten

On Main Street the hundreds of feet moving back and forth to school had reduced the snow to an ugly, treacherous slush, so we had to move slowly for fear of slipping. I carried Emily's books and lunch so she could concentrate on her pineapple.

Bobby went on ahead to scout the field. I think it was several acres; but at the moment it seemed as vast as a sea of pure, white milk.

When we reached him, he was crouching by the fence. "All clear," he whispered—as if Farmer Pynchon had extremely sensitive hearing.

We slipped our books and lunches between the railings, but Emily refused to let go of her pineapple which had now left orange spots over the front of her coat. Emily must have used watercolors.

"I'll have to climb up," she said.

Because of the danger, I felt like a messenger about to

make a dash across a wintry battlefield in France.

"Ready?" I asked.

"Ready," Bobby said grimly.

"Contact," Emily agreed from behind her pineapple.

"Then it's over the top." As I rose, I heard an imaginary whistle summoning the poor soldiers from their trenches.

Agile as a monkey, Bobby shinnied over the fence. He had already picked up his things and was beginning to trudge across the snow.

As I helped Emily ascend the fence railings, she called to him. "You wait up, Bobby, or you'll be sorry."

Pivoting, he backed along through the snow. "It's not my fault we're late. I was ready on time."

As she sat upon the top railing, Emily shook her pineapple at him. "Then you're getting a surprise for Christmas, but you aren't going to like it," Emily warned. "And I really mean it."

Bobby hesitated, because that was Emily's ultimate threat. Finally he began to trudge on back. "Okay, just this once."

"You're also getting heavy," I grunted. "No more double breakfasts for you."

"Careful," Emily warned, "or I'll fix you too."

"Lower the tankette," Bobby said, and caught her and the pineapple on the other side.

Trying to climb a fence decorously in my dress was difficult; and as I slid down from the top of the fence, I heard something tear.

Picking up Emily's and my own things, Bobby handed them to us. "One of your stockings is torn. It must have gotten caught on some nail. But you didn't get cut."

"At least you won't get lockjaw," Emily tried to console me. A classmate of hers had developed lockjaw after cutting himself on a rusty wire. For a month afterward, it had been Emily's main topic of conversation.

"If either of you had lockjaw, you'd explode with all the words you couldn't say," Bobby said as he left.

Emily pointed the pineapple top like the barrel of a cannon. "We'd better go, Joan."

She let me take the lead so I could flatten out the path that Bobby had already broken. He kept looking to his left and right as he went. Assured that he was keeping watch, we could concentrate on hurrying up to join him. Soon we were dogging his steps.

On the field, the snow had stayed deep. We could hear it grunt rhythmically beneath our galoshes. About halfway across the meadow, Emily chirped, "You're excused, Joan."

"For what?" I asked, looking over my shoulder.

Emily had set the pineapple on top of her head. "For making that noise. You must have made it, because it wasn't me."

I paused, but I could hear only the snow squeaking under Bobby's feet. "You must've heard Bobby."

"I was positive it was you," Emily argued. The pineapple bobbed up and down as she walked.

We hadn't gone more than three steps, though, when I did hear something. "Are you all right, Bobby?"

He plowed on through the snow like a wool-coated tugboat. "Of course I am—except for the fact I'm stuck with two sisters."

"We're the ones who are stuck with you," Emily jeered. She stopped when I did, nearly losing the pineapple in the process.

"What's the matter?" she asked, taking it in her arms again.

I turned slowly in a circle, trying to find the source of that mystery noise. I figured it couldn't be Farmer Pynchon. He would have been swearing a blue streak the way he normally did when he saw us trespassing.

I listened alertly and felt uneasy when I heard the loud snort.

Emily nudged me with the pineapple. "Joanie, tell me that was you."

When I shook my head, she asked Bobby, "Was it you, Bobby?"

Bobby shook his head too.

Suddenly I saw a dark shadow in the middle of the field, but before I could say anything, it disappeared. I stood on tiptoe, hoping it would help me see better. Cradling her precious pineapple in her arms, Emily pirouetted, trying to see what was wrong. "What is it?" she demanded.

"Something's out there." All I saw now was the snow drifting in little wisps before the wind like little ghostly snakes.

"Bobby," I said, "stop."

Bobby, however, was beyond patience. "What is it now?" he asked, as he kept on stamping through the snow.

Emily's mouth opened but no words came out. She

could only point her pineapple. I twisted sideways to look in the same direction. The wind grew stronger as a broad black back reappeared. The field itself lay on a gentle slope, so it must have been hidden in a fold of the land.

Bobby stared at the large dark blob. "It's Farmer Pynchon's horse, but I don't see Farmer Pynchon."

"I wonder if he fell off," I said.

Bobby turned and started to walk on. "It'd serve him right."

"You said there was nothing in the field," Emily scolded Bobby.

Bobby shrugged. "So sue me."

I kept watching, though. When it plowed closer, I saw, too late, that this horse had horns.

"Run, Emily. That's no horse. That's a bull." Shifting our books and lunches to one hand, I thrust out my other toward her.

"Wait," she said, shifting her pineapple into the crook of one arm so her other hand could take mine.

Emily began running without being told. "I knew we shouldn't have come this way. I knew it. I knew it." She held the pineapple like a football.

"Bobby, run," I called.

"What for?" When he turned around, his eyes grew wide. "Holy cow," he said, and took to his heels.

Behind us the bull gave a snort, and the ground began to pound as it started to trot after us.

"Now look what you did, Bobby," Emily panted. "When you called it a cow, you made it mad."

Bobby began floundering through the snow. "It's mad because we're in its pasture."

"Will you drop the pineapple?" I asked, exasperated.

Emily held on to it tighter. "And get an F? We'd lose Christmas for sure."

Half dragging Emily, I caught up with Bobby. "Farmer Pynchon must have put it here to keep us out."

When I looked behind me, I saw that the bull had broken into a gallop.

"Faster!" I shouted.

"Nice bully, bully, bully," Emily called to it in a high, desperate voice.

"It's not a dog. Run!" I jerked Emily along through the snow.

It was hard to move in the deep snow. We had to lift our legs very high to get them above the surface. Every step was such an effort that I felt like a fly in sticky syrup.

Bobby glanced over his shoulder. "It's gaining."

As my cap flew off, I took a quick peek behind me. The stream rose from its nostrils, so it seemed to move across the pasture like a small locomotive.

"Faster," I urged Emily.

Emily gave a wail when the green top of the pineapple snapped off against her chest. "Now look what you've done," she said in dismay.

The air was so cold that every breath felt as sharp-edged as a knife. I squinted over my shoulder. In that cold morning air, steam was rising from the bull's nostrils just like in the cartoons at the nickelodeon.

"It's getting closer," I said in a panic.

Somehow we picked up the pace. My lungs hurt now

with every breath. When I felt Emily slip, I yanked her back to her feet. "Come on," I ordered, and started to drag her, Emily protesting at every step.

"My pineapple," she said, and tried to jerk free so she could go back for the top.

"If you don't hurry, we'll bury your pineapple with you," I snapped.

"Maybe we can distract it," Bobby said. Turning his lunch bag upside down, he emptied the sandwich onto the snow. The rag bundle broke apart the moment it hit, scattering bread and baloney.

Emily jabbed her pineapple at me. "But what'll I eat at noontime?"

"You may not live till noontime." I let go of her hand long enough to empty out both our bags. Then, taking her hand, I began to run again with her.

The fence was only some ten paces away, but as we neared it, we hit a pocket of deeper snow. Suddenly every step became even more of an effort. When I looked in back, I saw that the bull had barely slowed to see what we had dropped.

Ahead of us Bobby leaned far forward, fighting through the waist-high snow toward the fence.

"Bobby, catch!" I called. When he turned around by the fence, I dropped our books and picked up Emily by the waist.

"Hey!" she said, kicking angrily.

I threw her with all my strength. She traveled only a couple of yards, but it was enough. Bobby seized her wrist and hauled her across the snow like an angry sled.

I whirled around and began waving my arms to draw

the bull's attention. "Hey, bull. Here, bull."

The sunlight glinted off the ring in the bull's nose as he charged. Still flapping my arms, I closed my eyes and waited for the impact.

The next instant, Bobby and Emily were shouting. "Run, Joan."

I opened my eyes to see the bull had stopped to stare at one of our sandwich rags, which was blowing across the snow. Grabbing the nearest bundle of books, I twisted around and began to stumble through the snow toward the fence where Bobby and Emily were waiting.

"Come on, Joan," Bobby called, throwing his books between the railings.

"You can do it," Emily encouraged.

Behind me the bull snorted, but I didn't dare look or ask what he was doing. The last three yards were the longest of my life, but I made it. Bobby had already climbed to the top of the fence and was helping Emily up by holding on to her armpits.

"Grip her tight," I warned him. Flinging the books between the railings, I grabbed Emily's ankles and hoisted her over the fence and onto the snow on the other side.

Bobby's eyes were so wide with fear now that they seemed to fill half of his face. "Joan." His voice shook.

I didn't waste time talking but stretched out my hand as I put my foot on the bottom railing. Bobby grabbed hold of my wrist and pulled as he fell over backward. At the same time I gave a kick with my foot on the bottom railing.

I felt myself clear the fence, and then I was falling

onto the other side with Bobby. Emily let out an angry squeal when we landed on top of her.

It wasn't a moment too soon. Behind me, the bull bellowed angrily, and I heard the fence rattle. As I rolled over onto my back, I saw the bull swing to its right in frustration. Its sharp hooves sent up clods of snow and icy dirt.

Bobby lay panting on the snow beside me. "That is one mean bull."

"That is one mean farmer." Emily sat up, trying to brush the snow from her coat. She looked a sight. So did we all.

We gave a jump when we heard a loud bang and snow fell from the top of the fence. We could see the angry dark shape between the fence railings. The fence shook again as it butted the fence with its head. It bellowed angrily.

"Do you think that fence will hold?" Emily asked with big eyes.

"I don't think we'll test it. Let's go." Getting up, I tried to dust the snow off.

Bobby retrieved the two bundles of books that had made it across. "I guess I can borrow half a sandwich from someone," Bobby said. He had a lot of friends in school.

"Janey'll share her lunch." Emily took one of the book bundles from Bobby.

I realized then that it must have been mine that got left in the field. Between me and them now stood a bull with wickedly sharp horns. "Mine are back in the pasture," I said.

"I can't even see my pineapple," Emily said, and began to cry.

"It was just a stupid pineapple," Bobby said. "Maybe your teacher will give you an extension on your homework."

Emily took a blind swat at Bobby. "I'm not crying for the pineapple. I'm crying about Christmas. I've lost any chance at my doll."

eleven

Then, with Bobby tugging Emily from in front and me pushing from behind, we made our way up the hill. The school bell began to ring. In the mood I was in, it sounded like the bells for a funeral.

Emily was in the same frame of mind. "Every year I have to listen to my friends talk about what they got for Christmas. I thought this year I would get to do some bragging too."

"We're lucky to be alive," Bobby reminded us. "I don't want to ever face the front end of a bull again."

"You weren't exactly facing the bull," Emily snickered.

I tried to head off another quarrel. "Bobby's right. There are a lot worse things than not getting a Christmas present. We could've had bones broken or worse."

"Now you're sounding like Mama," Emily grumbled.

"Scary, isn't it?" Bobby said.

Though it made me feel uncomfortable, I had to agree. "And I don't feel any better than when she says those kinds of things."

When we reached the schools, we parted company and I headed up the front steps of the high school.

The principal was waiting just within the doorway in a big cardigan sweater with bulging pockets. "*You're late, Joan.*"

I cringed because my principal was a match for any bull. My morning was getting more and more awful. "*I'm sorry, Miss Blake. I couldn't help it.*"

"*Well, you certainly didn't waste time before the mirror. You look as untidy as a scarecrow.*" She leaned forward to squint disapprovingly at me.

I dug a comb out of my coat pocket and blindly tried to repair my hair. "*I'm sorry, Miss Blake. We were . . . helping a friend of the family.*"

Miss Blake must have heard every sort of excuse in her time. "*What were you doing that left you in such a state?*"

I could feel my cheeks coloring. If I said Miss Lucy had kept us, I would have to explain how and why. And I was sure she wouldn't want that. "*I'm sorry, Miss Blake, but it's private.*"

I suppose she had dealt with so many sinners in her years that she found it hard to believe anyone was innocent. "*I see. Then you give me no choice. It's bad enough to be tardy, but to come to school in this state is disgraceful. Therefore I must assign you to detention after school.*"

I panicked at the thought. I'd never had detention

before this. My parents would not understand if I was late for that reason. Not only was Christmas lost, but Mama would never let me hear the end of it. *"Please, Miss Blake. I won't ever be late again. And I didn't dress this way for school. I was neat, but I was so late, I tried to take a shortcut and got chased by a bull."*

Miss Blake was not known to be merciful, but I suppose I looked so ragged and bedraggled that she felt sorry for me. *"Whose pasture was it?"*

I was afraid that she was going to report me, but I was too intimidated by Miss Blake to lie. *"Mr. Pynchon,"* I said. *"I think he put the bull there so we wouldn't trespass; but we didn't see it."*

Miss Blake tried to hide a smile. *"Hiram would shoot the sparrow that stole a kernel of corn. He's a man who knows what's his."*

"We were wrong, I know," I admitted.

"Well, you look like you've already had a year's growth scared out of you." She rose and fell on the balls of her feet. *"Are you going to do it again?"*

I shook my head most definitely. *"I'd rather tangle with you than the bull any day. I mean— "*

She held up a hand for me to be silent. *"I suppose that's a kind of compliment. So I'll settle for a two-hundred-word essay 'Why I Must Respect Fences'—due in a week."*

I almost kissed Miss Blake. *"Yes, ma'am."* Two hundred words would be no problem at all. The memory of those sharp horns would provide plenty of inspiration. *"I lost my books."*

"You'll have to pay for them. In the meantime I'll see

about getting new ones issued from the book depository."

That would do in Christmas for sure, and I thought despairingly of Emily and Miss Lucy. Mama and Papa could never forgive the expense. *"Yes, ma'am."*

She wrote out a pass and handed it to me. *"Freshen up first, Joan."*

I went to the girls' room and in the mirror saw that I was truly a sight. My hair had come undone, and my clothes were unkempt, and my cheeks were as red as raw steaks. Too late I remembered my torn stocking. You could see my bright-red union suit through the big hole.

Ann was the last thing I needed that day. She smirked as I passed her on the way to my seat in English class. Turning to one of her flock, she whispered loudly, *"I see England, I see France."*

To my chagrin, I felt my face begin to flush. *"Haven't you seen a union suit before?"* I hissed softly.

Ann's smile only grew broader. *"I was referring to yesterday, when you wrecked Mr. Barrington's automobile."*

I saw others smile in the class. The story had spread.

Seeing my distress, Victoria leaned toward me as I sat down. *"Pay it no mind. Father doesn't."*

I smiled at her gratefully. Victoria was the one real ray of sunshine on a gloomy day. She had a true gentility—not the kind that came with a castle and an official pedigree, but one that came from the heart. She liked to make people comfortable. I'd read in some farmer's almanac that that was the real definition of good manners.

Ann, though, was determined to relive every moment of yesterday's humiliation. *"I hope your father wasn't upset about what Joan did to his car."*

Victoria shook her head. *"My father says dents give it character—rather like dimples."* She turned to me and added, *"I just hope you've recovered from your accident."*

Victoria meant to comfort me, but her words only made me feel worse. I would never be the graceful creature Victoria was, nor would my father ever be Mr. Barrington. And I was sure their Christmases were equally as graceful and splendid. They were almost the exact opposites of us—especially now that I sat torn and dirty and thoroughly graceless.

"Yes, quite," I mumbled.

"Father will be so relieved," she said with a reassuring smile. *"I hope we didn't keep you up last night when we moved in. I didn't think we had so many things."*

"No," I fibbed. *"We were dead to the world."*

Suddenly she noticed my empty desk. *"But you have no books. Would you like to share mine?"*

"Victoria," Mr. Stevens asked, *"would you and Ann care to enlighten us?"*

Ann's face suddenly took on a very studious expression. *"It was nothing, sir."*

"It was a noisy kind of nothing," Mr. Stevens observed.

"We noticed that Joan doesn't have her book, so we asked her if she wanted to look on with one of us," Victoria said smoothly. I was grateful for the fib. The whole school probably knew about the incident yesterday, but I would just as soon not have it become a classroom topic.

At lunchtime I did not even look for Victoria, sure that she would be surrounded by Ann and the flock. Instead I went over and sat with Bernice, Havana, Henrietta, and Florie.

After yesterday I wondered how they would treat me; but their only concern was how I felt. And I blessed them for being such good friends.

So I got their advice on how to handle my parents over this Christmas catastrophe. I kept the question hypothetical, in the hope that they would not realize it was about my own family.

They were too smart for that; but they were polite enough to keep things also hypothetical. Florie had "modern" counsel from one of her slick magazines. Henrietta told me what one of her romance heroines would do—usually the proper thing to do. Havana had a relevant anecdote about a member of her large family—most of whom seemed to be suffering from bad luck of some sort. It was Bernice's common sense, however, that I most relied on.

However, Bernice broke off in mid sentence to stare over my shoulder in shock.

When I turned, I almost fell off the bench. Victoria was sitting down on my other side. *"It occurred to me, Joan, that if you lost your books, you might have lost your lunch as well. Would you like to share mine? After all,"* she said with a smile, *"yesterday you offered to share your baloney sandwich with me."* Her normal tone of voice was so quiet that it was almost lost in the din of the auditorium where we were all eating.

From a perfect little basket she produced a little square sandwich with the crusts off. It had been divided on the diagonal, and Victoria gave me half. Between hunger and curiosity, I was dying to bite into it; but I waited for her to begin eating and then copied her dainty nibblings. I tasted vegetables but little else; and it was all I could do to resist opening the sandwich to see what was inside.

Bernice didn't look any too happy to have the princess sitting with us, but Florie was starved for details about the new rich girl. "*Where did you go to school before this?*" she asked Victoria.

Victoria nibbled at a corner of her sandwich as if she had no appetite herself. "*I've gone to school here and there,*" she said vaguely. "*For a large part of the time, I've had my own tutors.*"

"*I hope this is not too much of a letdown,*" Bernice snapped, ready to pick a fight.

Victoria smoothly slid away from any unpleasantness such as an argument. "*How can it be, when everyone is so gracious?*"

Bernice glanced sideways at Victoria as if she suspected her of being sarcastic, but it was impossible to tell from Victoria's blank but polite expression.

"*Victoria,*" Ann called and waved, "*come over here.*"

For a second Victoria's mouth tightened and her eyes narrowed in irritation, but she covered up just as quickly. "*There's plenty of room here,*" Victoria told her.

Ann looked pointedly at Bernice. "*We . . . um . . . can't.*"

"I will go," Bernice said quietly.

"Then I'll go too," I said. I owed that much to my friend.

"And me," Henrietta said. She could be as determined a friend as she could be an interrogator. Of course, Florie and Havana chimed in too.

When we all started to rise, Victoria motioned for us to sit down again. *"Did I say something to offend you?"*

Bernice began to blush. *"No, it is the other way around. My parents are in the theater."* Many proper people frowned on theatrical folk.

"But I love the theater," Victoria protested. *"Are they actors?"*

Bernice blinked in surprise. *"Oh, dear, no. They are dancers and singers: the Terpsichorean Thrushes. And they usually get second billing with a box around their names."*

It took a moment for that to register with Victoria. *"I see,"* she said. Bernice and I got ready to leave; but Victoria added, *"You must tell me more."*

"Really?" Bernice asked. Besides me, Victoria was probably the only one who had ever wanted to know.

As it turned out, Bernice had been in almost as many big cities as Victoria. Besides New York there were Chicago and New Orleans, San Francisco and Seattle, and even a few Canadian cities. Afraid to call attention to herself, Bernice usually kept quiet about her travels.

In the meantime Ann and the flock did their best to pretend that they didn't miss Victoria, but I could tell they were straining to eavesdrop in that loud auditorium.

While they chatted, I kept waiting to hit some meat as

I ate, but there was nothing but greenery. When Bernice began telling some anecdote about a trained seal, I could resist no longer and lifted up the upper slice of bread. There was nothing but little green spots of . . .

"*Watercress,*" Victoria said, interrupting Bernice in mid story. Victoria had caught me peeking. "*I adore watercress sandwiches. I hope you don't mind.*"

"*But you're rich,*" Havana said, puzzled. "*Can't you afford meat?*"

Florie frowned. "*Oh, Havana. It's what all the elegant folk eat.*"

"*Well,*" Havana said stubbornly, "*if I could afford filet mignon for every meal, then that's what I'd have.*"

"*That's what the nouveaux riches would do,*" Florie said, and added with a whisper, "*like Ann. The truly genteel don't flaunt it just because they have the money.*"

Even so, part of me agreed with Havana. I had once been embarrassed because all my family had to eat were lettuce sandwiches. So meatless sandwiches were a symbol of poverty to me. It was a small thing, but it made me think again how different she was from me.

I put the slices together again. "*It was good enough for Peter Rabbit.*"

Victoria smiled brightly. "*That's the furry little fellow.*"

"*Any chamomile tea?*" I asked, glancing at her basket.

"*Just the ticket!*" Victoria pretended to agree, and then leaned forward to whisper confidentially, "*Though it makes me frightfully sleepy. What about you?*"

"*I've had plenty of different kinds of Chinese teas,*" I said, "*but never chamomile.*"

"It's the perfect thing before bed," Victoria advised, *"but in my thermos I have Earl Grey. What are Chinese teas like?"*

"There are all kinds. Black teas. Green teas." I remembered a can on the kitchen shelf. *"Even something called Dragon Well tea."*

Victoria considered that for a moment and then opined, *"I'm sure the tea must be as delightful as the name. So poetical."*

"I had a teacher once who read us a story by Cyrano de Bergerac," Havana said. She loved fantasy novels. *"In it Cyrano flew to the moon, where poems were the official currency."*

"I'd be a pauper there," Victoria confessed.

"So would I," Havana said. *"And the moon people never ate. Instead, they went into rooms filled with flowers and inhaled the fragrance."*

I had heard the story before. *"I always think of Cyrano when I drink jasmine tea."*

"You'll think me terribly gauche, but I've never had jasmine tea," Victoria said.

It surprised me that there was anything I might have had that she hadn't. *"But you have to try it,"* I said, liking her even more now. *"You'd love it."*

"Thank you, Joan," Victoria said. *"I'd love to have tea with you. I know—why don't I come home with you today? Since you don't have your books, we can do our homework together."*

I hesitated at first. After London and Geneva I wasn't sure what she would make of our laundry. There was such a great gap between us.

It wasn't that I was ashamed of my parents or our laundry. They were good, hardworking people; but I knew they would be out of place with Victoria. In fact, I felt ashamed of myself for just thinking those things.

"*And then,*" Victoria went on, "*as my reward, I can have some of your jasmine tea. I'm dying to try it.*"

I shouldn't have worried about Victoria. She wouldn't look down her nose at us even if our cups weren't Wedgwood and our furniture wasn't Chippendale. And then I realized that with a guest there, my parents would have to temper their scolding. Things might even work out after all.

For the first time that day I began to feel real hope. "*That's one curiosity I can satisfy.*"

Victoria had barely touched her half of the sandwich, and she deposited the rest of it in her basket. "*Joan, perhaps the other part of my lunch will be more to your taste?*"

From the basket she lifted out a small bundle wrapped in a cloth napkin. When she spread it open, we saw a pale-yellow wedge of cheese, which she held up lovingly between her fingers. "*This is Appenzeller. It's bathed in vats of wine by cheerful monks.*"

Henrietta drew her head back suspiciously, as if it were contaminated. Her family were strict temperance people who never touched alcohol. "*Will it make you drunk?*"

Victoria fought more or less successfully not to smile. "*No, the alcohol's all gone. It just has a nice, fruity taste.*"

She broke off bits and handed them around. Beyond us Ann was rising from her seat to see what was going on. When we had sampled the cheese, Florie shook her head. *"I don't know if I would call it fruity."*

I tried to be polite. *"But it does have a . . . a tang."*

Victoria generously broke the remaining cheese into halves and presented me with the larger one. *"Then the monks' labors were not in vain."*

And then from her magical basket she drew a delicious orange. The cheese was a marvel enough, but we all gaped at the sight of the fruit resting on her palm. In the winter the only fruit that was around had been dried or bottled or canned from the summer before. So the sight of fresh fruit was as miraculous as if she had plucked a rose from out of a snowbank. *"Where did you get it here?"* I wondered.

Bernice had picked up the orange to admire it. *"Yes, I would also like to know where you get fresh oranges in the winter."*

"Father asked and then just . . . obtained it." She gave a little shrug.

I marveled at someone who could take such magic matter-of-factly. Fruit of any kind was hard to get in the winter. They might have it in California or Florida, but it was hard to ship it here—and what little trickled in came with a hefty price tag.

Simply to wish for something and your father got it for you—it was a life I would never know. I could only sit and imagine. And envy.

Every day was Christmas for Victoria.

twelve 

After school Mr. Barrington was outside the building, leaning jauntily against his automobile. Already with him were Ann and her flock. Victoria indicated me as we walked up. *"Father, you remember Joan."*

A tip of the hat and a glance of the piercing blue eyes. *"How could I forget the human battering ram? What's on your agenda today? Demolishing a tank or two?"*

Cringing inwardly, I inspected his car for signs of damage but was amazed to find they had disappeared. *"What happened to the dent?"*

He waved a hand breezily. *"I had a fellow work on it overnight. Couldn't have my daughter be ashamed of our car."*

Victoria pretended to pout. *"But you said the dent gave our car character."*

"You know how whimsical I am," he said, and then

doffed his hat to Ann. "*Miss Wood here has kindly invited us to high tea.*"

Ann fussed with her coat collar. "*It's so very hard to have a proper tea here. But we try to keep up the standards. We'll even have clotted cream. We became quite fond of high tea when my English cousin visited us two summers ago.*"

"*It sounds like a delightful repast,*" Mr. Barrington said.

Victoria made a point of reaching out and touching my wrist. "*Joan and I were going to study together.*" She pleaded silently with her eyes for me to support her story. And I realized with a start that she didn't like Ann any more than I did.

"*Yes, we were,*" I said, and was rewarded with a grateful wink from Victoria.

Ann scowled. "*Joan can come too.*"

I was startled at first, but I suddenly realized that if I went, I would be able to see how the Woods lived. I imagined a huge mansion with glass chandeliers. And servants! Plenty of them. And we would dine off china so fine that it would be thin as paper and ring like a bell. And it would be a real English tea like in the books. While I didn't relish having to spend an afternoon with Ann, I was curious about her house and the way the rich lived.

It would be like picking berries with Miss Lucy. Ann's tongue was as sharp as any bramble, and so you had to expect to get stabbed a few times. But there was always the fruit to savor.

After this morning a social tea was just as much out

of reach as Christmas. *"I wish I could,"* I said regretfully, *"but it's quite out of the question."*

Ann blinked in surprise; I don't think many people refused her invitations. But then she looked relieved. *"What a pity."*

Mr. Barrington leaned his head to the side. *"What shall we do? I accepted an invitation from Ann, and you accepted one from Joan."* However, his tone made it plain that he thought Victoria should choose Ann. After all, she was of their class and I was a lowly peasant.

Ann pressed her lips together in a thin, tight line. She must have been thinking along the same lines. *"Well, I really don't think it's fair to keep Victoria from going, do you?"*

"Oh, no," Victoria said stubbornly. *"I couldn't think of deserting Joan."* She pressed my hand, begging silently again for support. *"Could I, Joan?"*

"You understand, don't you, Joan?" Mr. Barrington asked.

I reminded myself of how generous he had been about the car. I had to be equally generous now in the only way I could. *"I really don't want to spoil your afternoon,"* I said.

Ann pounced immediately. *"There, you see?"*

Victoria squeezed my hand harder. *"It won't. A promise is a promise. You lost your books."*

I wondered if my fingertips were turning blue from lack of circulation. Against my better judgment, I said, *"If you're sure—"*

Victoria said to Ann. *"Do forgive me."*

"Certainly," Ann said, without an ounce of sincerity in her voice at all.

However, Mr. Barrington snapped his fingers. "*I have it, Victoria. You can lend her your books and then pick them up after the tea.*"

Victoria took hold of my arm. "*As much as I would like to come to tea, I think I should keep my promise.*"

Mr. Barrington cleared his throat. "*But Ann has made such a great effort already.*"

Victoria smiled sweetly. "*Then you should definitely go, Father.*"

"*But it won't be the same without you,*" Ann insisted.

Mr. Barrington looked uncomfortable. I guess he didn't like denying his daughter anything. "*Well, this is a bit of a dilemma, isn't it? But I think the honorable thing would be to visit the one who has gone to so much trouble to please you.*"

"*It was ever so hard to find some of these things here,*" Ann said.

"*I'm sorry to cause you so many problems, but you should have consulted me first,*" Victoria said.

Ann glared at me. "*Joan, you wouldn't want to spoil Victoria's fun.*" It was her own and not Victoria's pleasure that Ann had in mind.

Though I didn't want to grant Ann another victory, I also felt I owed Mr. Barrington. If he wanted Victoria to attend a tea with Ann, then I wouldn't stand in his way.

Gently I disengaged myself from her grasp. "*No, it's quite all right. If you'll just let me borrow your books . . .*"

Victoria looked disappointed. "*Are you sure you don't mind?*"

Trying to ignore Ann's gloating face, I held out my hands for Victoria's books. "*Of course not.*"

"Some other time then," Victoria said, reluctantly passing her books to me.

Mr. Barrington tipped his hat to me gratefully and then took Victoria's hand. *"Come, my dear."*

"I'll stop by later, Joan," Victoria said as he led her around the automobile.

"I'll have the books ready," I promised.

Ann got into the front seat. The rest of her flock roosted around her. Mr. Barrington tooted his horn, and the automobile played the notes of a hunting call. *"We're forever in your debt."* He swung his automobile slowly out into the street. His tire hit a depression where a slushy pond had formed, and the weight of the car sent the muddy slush sailing all over me. I tried to wipe the smudge away with my hand, but I was now a total disaster. What the bull hadn't messed up, Mr. Barrington had just taken care of.

It didn't help my mood any that Ann had turned around in the front seat and was silently laughing at me.

Wallowing in self-pity, I floundered angrily through the deep snow until I caught up with Emily and Bobby. They were high-stepping through the snow in their galoshes.

"When I told my teacher what happened, she said I could turn in my pineapple later," Emily said.

"Good," I grunted. I was glad that one of us had done all right today.

A piece of paper fell out of one of Emily's books and when I picked it up, I saw a series of triangles she had drawn in pencil. "What's that?"

"A Christmas tree," she snapped, as if I should have

known. "Even if I can't have Christmas, I can send out Christmas cards." And she snatched it back and stowed it back in her books.

We didn't say anything the rest of the way home. The snow had fallen from the trees before the laundry, so they were once again bare skeletons, and the snow had turned into an ugly gray slush so it matched our mood perfectly. It didn't seem like the world would ever be green again.

I stared at the freshly shoveled steps with dread. "Let's get the torture over with." I climbed them slowly toward the inquisition.

Opening the front door, I let Emily and Bobby file by and then followed them inside the laundry. Mama and Papa were both behind the counter as I stepped inside.

Farmer Pynchon was there talking to my parents. He was a big man—he filled the space like a stove dressed in a flannel coat and blue bib coveralls.

"Uh-oh," Emily said as she eased in behind me.

Farmer Pynchon had taken off his hat, which he tapped against his hip. *"I'm a man of few words, so I'll be quick and to the point. I came to complain about your children. They got my bull so riled with their teasing that it took me most of the day to get him back into my barn. That put me behind on my chores, and it took me so long to do 'em that the roast chicken was like string because my wife had to keep my dinner warm for so long. And I'm a man who needs to keep up his strength."*

"A few words, huh?" Emily whispered to me.

Farmer Pynchon plowed on relentlessly. *"Now, I'm not an ogre, and I was a youngster myself. And in my prime I was a real rascal and the terror of the county. If anyone can take a prank, it's me.*" It took him a couple of minutes to get around to the point. "*You got to keep your youngsters in control.*"

"*We're sorry we trespassed,*" I said quickly, hoping to avert a real catastrophe.

"*It don't matter.*" He shook his head firmly. "*Habits are habits, and if you get into the habit of sashaying across my land, then you'll forget come the spring.*"

Mama had squeezed her eyebrows together as she strained to make out the conversation. Papa had given up completely and was simply glancing between Mama and Farmer Pynchon as he waited for a translation from Mama.

"*How you know my children tease your bull?*" Mama demanded. "*You see them?*"

"*Well, no, but I found these books,*" he said, opening the gunny sack on the counter.

It was all the proof he needed; but at least I wouldn't have to pay for a new set.

However, what he took out was a nest of paper. The books were all torn up—as if the bull must have personally stomped them into the snow.

Scattered among the pages were wet orange lumps—the remains, I suppose, of Emily's creation. "*I can't figure out what that was,*" Mr. Pynchon said, pointing at one scrap. "*Me and the missus've been puzzling over that the whole day.*"

Emily prodded one piece curiously. "*It used to be my homework. I made a pineapple out of papier-mâché.*"

"*Fancy that,*" Mr. Pynchon said. "*I would've liked to see that before it landed in the snow.*"

When Mama raised the cover of the first book, it came off in her hand. And there was my homework. "We brought you children up to respect other people's property," Mama said without looking at us.

"They led my bull on a merry chase all over," Farmer Pynchon went on. *"I've seen the tracks myself. They're all over the field. It was a one-bull stampede."*

Papa nudged Mama, but she put up a hand as she tried to get to the bottom of things. *"My children go in your field and bull in field too?"*

"Yessum," Farmer Pynchon said. *"That bull was there as plain as day, so I thought it was sure to keep them out of there. But they deliberately went in."*

"It was hidden by a fold of land," I tried to explain, but I could feel the ground begin to slide out from underneath me.

Mama became stone-faced. "So you admit it."

"If we could have seen it, we wouldn't have entered," I tried to argue.

Farmer Pynchon looked back and forth during this exchange, guessing at the subject. *"Next time your youngsters might not be so lucky."*

"Yes," Mama said. *"We sorry. Not happen again."*

Mama nodded her thanks and then motioned to Papa. He copied her obediently. Then she began explaining to him in Chinese.

Helplessly I listened to them, wanting to defend myself but unable to get a word in edgewise. I watched in apprehension as Papa's face grew angrier and angrier as he listened to Mama.

When Mama was done, Papa bowed even more

deeply this time to Farmer Pynchon. "*We sorry. These bad, bad children.*"

"*They ain't so bad. Like I said, I was a regular rascal.*" He held his hat away from his hip. "*And look at how successful I've become.*"

As Mama and Papa escorted him to the door, I examined the books. "They're beyond saving," I said in disappointment, and I waited for the parental storm to break.

I was just glad Victoria was not here. Compared to her indulgent father, my parents would have mystified her.

thirteen

When they turned around again, Mama's and Papa's lips were pressed tightly together and their eyebrows were narrowed. Sure signs of trouble.

Emily immediately pointed at our brother. "It was all Bobby's fault," Emily said, trying to defend me. "He said the coast was clear."

I signed for Emily to keep quiet. "We couldn't help being late, Papa. Miss Lucy wanted to show us her Christmas preparations, and that made us late."

"I know. That's why I got you this morning." Papa began rubbing his stomach sourly, as if he had a stomachache.

Sometimes I felt as if I had my left foot on one galloping horse and my right foot on another—and both were getting ready to gallop in separate directions. "Punish me, then, but not Bobby and Emily. I'll work through Christmas Day with you, but let them celebrate with Miss Lucy."

"You're all bad children. Why should any of you have Christmas?"

I remembered how nostalgic Miss Lucy had been this morning. "But Miss Lucy's counting on it," I said. "She has no family."

"I've just about had my fill of that busybody. She just spoils you and makes you misbehave," Papa said sternly. "Look at your clothes. And your books! Your school trusted you with those books." He looked at me as if I had betrayed my best friends. His angry face was a marked contrast to Mr. Barrington's.

I remembered how Mr. Barrington had found scarce fruit for his daughter in the dead of winter. He wouldn't have begrudged the cost of a few old clothes and textbooks. "I'll pay for them somehow," I said. "Maybe Miss Lucy will have odd jobs for me."

From the corner of my eye I saw Emily slip outside. I hadn't expected her to desert me like a little coward—not when I needed her the most.

"But the worst is that you endangered your little brother and sister," he said to me. Papa's cheeks grew flushed as he glared at me. "You're the eldest, so you're responsible for the safety of the little ones."

That was too much. "What really worries you? Our safety or your reputation?"

"Your mother and I didn't come to this barbaric country just so some witless fool could endanger her little brother and sister," Papa shouted.

Even though I was still afraid, I was angry and frustrated that I had missed an afternoon with the Barringtons. And I was also getting tired of being insulted by one of the people who ought to forgive me. If Farmer Pynchon had complained to Mr. Barrington about Victoria, he would have defended her or at least sympathized.

I felt betrayed, and that made me just as angry as Papa. "Will you hear our side of it, Papa?"

However, Papa slapped his hand on the counter. "You need to spend less time with your American friends and more time with Master Kung. From now on, all of you just stay in the laundry. It's time you became proper Chinese."

That seemed like the final injustice. "We hardly ever get to do any activities after school, so I don't know what you're complaining about. Besides, Master Kung's too old-fashioned even for China. That's why they abolished all those exams about all that kind of stuff. It's not like it's getting us ready to go back to China. China's changed a lot since you left. China's modernizing. They want people with engineering degrees."

Papa's head snapped back as if I had slapped him. "Is that what they teach you in the American schools: to talk back to your father?"

I was destroying any chance for future Christmases, but I was past caring. All the injustices of the past boiled up inside me in a dark, bitter flood. "You ought to know what I learn. You interrogate me every day."

Papa stiffened. "I'm your father."

"Maybe I'm tired of being interrogated," I said resentfully.

Mama always got this funny look when I argued with her and Papa—as if her mind were working at a faster speed than normal and all the mental energy was about to make her explode; almost as if she were an overstuffed chair about to burst the seams.

Even when we used Chinese, it was hard for Mama to follow our logic sometimes. "Tired?" she repeated, as if she were unsure I had really said that. "How can you be tired? We do all the work."

I shook my head. "We do twice the work of any of our classmates."

Mama slapped her hand on the table. "That's because they're lazy."

Miss Lucy's voice floated down the hallway. *"Hello, neighbors."* She was trying hard to sound cheerful, but she couldn't mask all her anxiety.

Papa threw up his hands in exasperation. "What does she want now? Why is she invading our home?"

"I'll tell her to come back later," Mama said, turning to head off her friend.

Emily appeared first, towing Miss Lucy after her into the kitchen. I realized that my little sister hadn't been a coward. She'd gone to get reinforcements.

Emily looked anxiously over her shoulder at Miss Lucy as a prompt. Miss Lucy cleared her throat self-consciously. *"I understand the children have been misbehaving."*

"They bad. Very bad." Papa shook his head for emphasis.

Miss Lucy put her hands comfortingly on Emily's shoulders. *"Emily told me about the contest. That seems rather extreme to me."*

Papa took Emily and tugged her away from Miss Lucy's grasp. *"That our business."*

"You really ought to give them a second chance," Miss Lucy argued. *"They're just children."*

The words just exploded from Papa, as if he'd been nursing a grudge for a long time. *"What you know about children?"* he demanded.

"Well, I taught school for several decades—" Miss Lucy began.

"But you not have your own," Papa blurted angrily.

"Papa!" I said, shocked at his rudeness.

Miss Lucy's head twitched back on her neck, and she was silent for a moment while she tried to control her hurt and her anger. *"It's true, but I have educated several generations of children."*

Papa had more angry thoughts than his English could express. Frustrated, he wound up slapping his chest. *"They our children. Not yours. Ours."*

When Miss Lucy seemed on the point of crying, I couldn't stay on the riverbank anymore but waded in. "Don't pick on Miss Lucy," I said in Chinese.

For a moment Papa looked at me so furiously that I thought he was going to slap me. "You stay out of this. She has no business interfering."

"Miss Lucy is our friend," I insisted. "In fact, she's more than a friend. She's family." I tried to enlist my mother's aid. "Isn't she, Mama?"

Mama was torn between her husband and her best

friend. "She has done us many favors."

Miss Lucy had been puzzled and even afraid by the angry exchange in Chinese. *"Please speak English."*

"I speak what I want. I pay rent." Papa started to stab his index finger all around him. *"This my house. My children."*

Miss Lucy glanced at the worried Emily, and that gave her the courage not to back down. "*Who should have what all the other children have. How can you be so heartless?*"

However, that was the final straw for Papa. "*Christmas make children bad. Make lazy.*" He glared at me. *"They talk back. No Christmas now. No Christmas ever."*

When Emily and Bobby started to cry, Miss Lucy gathered them both in her arms. "*Of all the mean, spiteful men . . . You remind me of Scrooge.*"

I don't think Papa knew who Scrooge was. Still, he could sense it was an insult. *"And you busybody. Witch. Cow. Republican,"* he spluttered. His limited English gave him little ammunition in the way of insults.

I stepped between Papa and Miss Lucy. "Stop it, Papa."

Mama put her hand between my shoulder blades and gave me a little shove. "The more you open your mouth, the more you prove your father is right. Apologize to your father," she ordered in Chinese.

As afraid as I was, though, I was not about to bend. "No."

"I won't have my children defying—" Suddenly, Papa stiffened and grew pale.

Mama ran to tend Papa. "You're upset because you're not feeling well."

Papa's voice was strained as he doubled over in pain. "Tell that woman and the children to leave."

"Are you all right, Mr. Lee?" Miss Lucy asked, suddenly solicitous.

Mama made shooing motions with her hands as she walked toward us. Bobby and Emily hesitated fearfully and then went upstairs, but I lingered, suddenly sorry for Papa.

He winced as he rubbed his stomach. "The children are giving me an ulcer," he said to Mama.

"You have a lot of responsibilities," Mama said soothingly.

Miss Lucy had forgotten their feud. Though she couldn't understand them, it was obvious Papa was in pain. *"Maybe a nice glass of warm milk would help,"* she suggested.

"Does your stomach hurt much, Papa?" I asked, sorry I had quarreled with him.

Mama massaged his back. "Your father doesn't want to worry you children, so he's been hiding his troubles. But he's been vomiting and has diarrhea most of the time."

"You don't have to tell Joan all that. It's embarrassing," Papa winced.

"You've hardly slept at all," Mama protested.

When I heard that, I felt worse about some of the things I had been thinking. "I didn't realize." Even if I was innocent, I didn't mean to increase Papa's pain. And when I thought about it, I should have been more careful. "I'm sorry, Papa. I'll try to read Master Kung. And we won't ever go near Farmer Pynchon's farm again."

He remained bent over as he gave me a weak smile. "I know."

Miss Lucy leaned toward Papa. *"I'll get a doctor."*

Papa hated a fuss. He tried to straighten, but the pain was too great and he bowed his head again. *"No American doctor,"* he commanded hoarsely.

"Miss Lucy will know a good one," Mama urged. "Her grandfather was a doctor."

Papa shook his head. "Western doctors are nothing but quacks. They know nothing about the life force or how to harmonize the body's humors."

"Then some warm milk?" Mama suggested.

"That will be fine," Papa said, and winced.

"He really should see a doctor," Miss Lucy said, studying Papa.

Mama smiled bravely at her friend. *"Maybe better you go."*

"But— " Miss Lucy tried to protest.

Mama put a hand on her friend's back and shoved gently. *"Please."*

Miss Lucy started to leave reluctantly. *"Very well, but don't hesitate to send one of the children if you need me."*

Then Mama and I helped Papa to the kitchen. After we had helped him sit on a stool, I went to the icebox that Miss Lucy had given us when she had gotten a new one. Taking out the bottle of milk, I poured some into a pot and then put the bottle back into the icebox. "Maybe Miss Lucy will let us use her phone so we can call Uncle Bing and ask him to get advice from a Chinese doctor." Uncle Bing lived up in Pittsburgh where there was a small number of Chinese.

Papa had gripped the table, but he waved me away when I tried to go to him. "And have that fool tell everyone between here and China?"

While the milk heated up on the stove, Mama started to reach for the teacups in a high cabinet. "You're as stubborn as Joan."

Papa gritted his teeth. "She gets it from me." He tried to laugh, but his insides hurt too much.

Since Papa wouldn't let me help him, I went over to help Mama. With my longer reach, it was easier for me to get them down from the shelf. "Mama," I whispered, "we really have to do something."

Mama sighed. "Right now, he's so worked up, he wouldn't listen to anyone." She arranged three cups on the table.

Just before the milk started to boil, I got a pot holder and lifted the pot from the stove. When I tilted the pot over the first cup, the steaming milk hissed as it touched the hot metallic lip and then fell in a frothy cascade into the cup.

Papa sipped the milk. "I don't know if my father would believe I would drink this greasy stuff. We never drank milk in China."

At the first taste of the warm milk, I began to feel sleepy myself. "You were missing out on a treat."

He cradled the cup in his hands, staring at the tiny white bubbles. "There were no dairy products at all. No milk or cheese."

"Or ice cream," I said. Miss Lucy had made some last summer. Though it was a chore to break up the ice and then turn the crank, the result had been delightful.

"The Chinese had ice cream too," Papa said. "But it was more like flavored ice."

"I'll take ice cream any day," I said, finishing my milk.

"That's one thing I'll miss when we go home," Papa admitted. "I'm going to bed."

Mama took my cup. "I'll clean up. You should do your homework before supper."

As I got up, Papa smiled and nodded a good night. "Joan, don't tell the little ones about my ulcer. Tell them I just had a little bellyache."

I put my hands on his shoulders. "I think they should know."

He put his hands up to cover mine. "Not yet. Let them think their papa is still indestructible."

It was a compliment, in a way, that he admitted his weakness to me. It meant I was more grown-up than Bobby and Emily. But his confession also made me feel sad.

I couldn't help hugging Papa then—though it was something neither he nor Mama encouraged—because I had suddenly realized something. "But that means we should love you all the more, because you need it."

Papa never took a compliment well. "There's plenty

of time for them to know the truth about their papa. Let . . . let them feel safe for a little while longer."

I wondered what I would have done if I had been in my parents' place—in a strange land as I tried to raise three children in an even stranger culture. I wasn't sure if I would have done half as well as they had, and I felt so sad for them that I had to hug Mama too. She returned the embrace and then pushed me away. "Hurry up and do your homework."

The warm milk made me feel drowsy, but I got through my homework and supper—though I did it a bit more quickly than I would have liked. My eyelids felt as if they were weighted with stones, so I gave up waiting for Victoria to come by for her books.

Somehow, though, I made it into my bedroom, where Emily already lay asleep—a little bump under the bed quilt. I got undressed and changed into my nightgown, hurrying in the cold air. Then, padding barefoot over the icy floor, I crept into the bed beside her.

Emily had been waiting for me to get in so she could "spoon" herself against me—as she called it. Drowsily she pressed her back against me, fitting herself to me—which would have been fine except for her feet were still as cold as icicles. "Is Papa okay?"

I felt ages older as I remembered Papa's request. "Papa's fine. It's just a little stomach trouble."

"What kept you so long?"

As we lay on our sides, feeling our bodies heat up my part of the quilt gradually, I looked at the stark silhouette of the trees that the streetlamps cast on the windows. "We were just talking."

Emily murmured as she snuggled in closer. "About what?" Her face, so pale and round, turned to face me.

"Things."

Emily yawned. "Like what?"

Under the heavy quilt I swung my feet away from her icy ones. "It was nothing." At least nothing she needed to know.

Emily's cold feet relentlessly pursued mine. "You didn't fight with Papa again?"

"No," I reassured her, and in a moment I could hear her soft, even breathing and feel the warm, rhythmic pulsations of her breath.

And pretty soon I was asleep too, and dreaming that I was lost in the middle of a winter storm. The wind was whipping the snow from the ground, mingling it with the flakes falling from the sky. I was lost in a whole world of white, and I became so confused that I couldn't tell where my feet and head ought to be.

When I saw a shadowy shape in front of me, I tried to open my mouth to call but nearly choked on all the snow. The shadow kept getting closer and closer. Suddenly I saw it was our snowwoman. The lumps of coal that were her eyes had a slick, oily gleam, and her mouth was fixed in a harsh smile.

I tried to turn and run, but my legs were fixed to the ground as if the snowwoman had stolen the power of motion from me. When she opened her tree-branch arms, I could not even scream.

As she wrapped her limbs around me, I could feel her coldness. The chill stabbed straight into my bones. She kept pressing against me until I felt like I was smothering in another snowbank; snow was oozing into my very flesh, and the snowwoman and I were fusing into one body. By the time I tried to protest, it was already too late, for my mouth—like the rest of my body—was white, frozen snow.

I ached with the cold until even my souls turned into ice.

fourteen

I slept poorly that night. I felt guilty about Papa's stomach trouble. While I wasn't the sole cause of his ulcer, I certainly hadn't helped it any. And in the last few days I had definitely made it worse.

When morning came, I made myself get up though I still felt tired. I was going to do my best to make Papa feel better. When Mama peered in the door, I was already washing up at the basin on top of the dresser. "We had the same idea," she said approvingly.

I smiled back. "If we get an early start to school, there won't be any trouble." In a low voice so Emily couldn't hear, I asked, "How did Papa sleep?"

Mama just shook her head. "Not good. Will you talk to Bobby and Emily about Christmas? I'm sure their pestering doesn't help his stomach."

Mama was always leaving the unpleasant jobs to me. "Without telling them about his ulcer?" I asked.

Mama dropped her eyes. "They'll listen to you."

Mama used that as an excuse whenever she passed on an unpleasant job to me. It didn't strike me as being fair. However, she had enough to deal with, so I wasn't about to begin another quarrel. As Mama hurried from the room, I turned to wake Emily.

For once Emily managed to dress herself. Of course, she put on her sweater backward, and then when I took it off her, I found that she had gotten all the buttons wrong on her dress. But I appreciated her attempt to help. Bobby was already waiting in the hallway, kicking his heel against the wall as he waited.

When we trooped downstairs, Papa was eating his usual breakfast of rice gruel. However, as a concession to Miss Lucy, he was drinking milk instead of hot tea. "How are you, Papa?" I asked anxiously. "Did you sleep well?"

Papa was all smiles, but there were dark spots under his eyes, as if he had not slept well. "Of course," he said loudly for Emily and Bobby's benefit. And then when they were busy getting their breakfast, he whispered to me, "Now remember. Don't say anything to the little ones."

"I promise," I said, and gave him a quick peck on the cheek.

After the last few days, it seemed strange to have a leisurely breakfast and take our time making our sandwiches. It seemed even stranger to be traveling with everyone else in school instead of staggering along by ourselves because we were late. We joined the stream of children trudging sluggishly up the hill.

I figured that now was as good a time as any to get the unpleasantness over with. "You know," I said to Bobby and Emily, "maybe we shouldn't worry about Christmas this year."

Emily squared her shoulders as if getting ready for battle. "But the bull wasn't really our fault. Miss Lucy made us late."

"I know," I said. Not being able to tell them about Papa's condition was like trying to run with one foot in a bucket. "But I think they're more upset than they let on. Why don't we wait till next year, when we can plan our campaign better."

Emily looked at me as if I had betrayed her. "If you don't believe in something, it won't happen. All my life I've been waiting for Christmas. I'm not going to quit now. And what about Miss Lucy? She's looking forward to it."

I felt a twinge of conscience. You ought to be able to do the right thing without hurting anyone. "She'll just have to understand," I said lamely.

"Then she can explain it to me, because I don't," Emily snapped. She made a point of moving away to join a group of her friends. Somehow she didn't have any trouble keeping the pace when she was with her classmates. I heard them begin to talk excitedly about their school's Christmas party, because tomorrow Christmas vacation began.

Desperate, I appealed to Bobby. "Talk to Emily, will you?"

Bobby also stared at me as if I were a traitor. "She won't listen to me." He shrugged sullenly and stalked over to his own friends and also began to talk about the party.

Obviously appealing to their better nature was not going to work. I would have to be more clever when I made the next try; but as I walked up to my school alone, I couldn't come up with one thing. It made me feel very old and tired and stupid.

When I got to school, there was a small mob around Ann and the flock who were talking about the marvelous tea. Gritting my teeth, I went over to Victoria. *"I was expecting you to pick your books up last night."*

Victoria smiled apologetically. *"Something came up."*

I held them out. *"Here. Your books saved my life."*

Victoria seemed glad to have someone besides the flock to talk to. *"I'm so glad. Did you sip jasmine tea and think of Monsieur de Bergerac?"*

I thought of Master Kung. *"Not quite. How did you get your homework done?"*

"After tea I did it with Ann." Victoria pressed her lips together, as if that were a whole story in itself. *"Someday I'd like to try some jasmine tea. I'm sure that one sip of the elixir and I shall be spouting poetry too."* Victoria had a slight smile, as if she were about to begin one of her flights of fancy.

Ann, however, cut it short so she could rub yesterday in. *"Sorry you couldn't have tea with us, Joan. You missed a swell time."*

Good old Bernice swept over and immediately leaped to my defense. *"'Swell' is so vulgar. Don't you think, Ann?"* Bernice asked loudly.

Ann tilted up a dimpled chin. *"You would know*

about all sorts of vulgarities. Wouldn't you, Bernice?"

"I know about you," Bernice stated with simple dignity.

Realizing that she was outgunned and outclassed in a battle of wits, Ann merely sniffed. *"Mother was delighted, you know. Victoria and I took so long to do our homework that I had her and her father stay for dinner. Mr. Barrington was charming at the table, and she talked him into taking a position with my father."*

I thought it odd that with all his talents, Mr. Barrington would take a job in his grandfather's former bank. *"How . . . nice. I'm sure he'll like working in his grandfather's old office."*

Ann tittered. *"Goose, what would a clerk be doing in an office?"*

It must have been humiliating to be a simple clerk in the very bank his grandfather had once owned. It especially seemed strange for a man who drove such a fancy automobile and who bought such fancy clothes and traveled all over Europe. Ann's father was probably crowing about it just as much as his daughter was.

Similar thoughts were going through the minds of others. I couldn't help glancing at Victoria, and I saw her cheeks burning red with embarrassment. I took that as confirmation.

"It's Father's way of understanding our family roots. He's so . . . thorough," Victoria murmured. *"It's just temporary, you understand."*

"And he may not remain a clerk," Ann hinted with a wink at Victoria. *"You and I will both work on my father."* A possible promotion would be the carrot that

would keep both Barringtons in harness.

Victoria stood there helplessly, all poetry and flights to the moon vanished. She could only listen to Ann chattering on about all the things Ann could do for her father. I was glad when Bernice touched my arm to leave.

As we moved away, I said to Bernice, "*Thank you for defending me.*"

"*The newly rich are like that,*" Bernice said. "*I once knew a trained seal act that rose up the vaudeville circuit to play the Hippodrome in New York. He liked to stick his nose up in the air just like Ann, but he still smelled of fish.*"

It was terrible, but I couldn't resist asking, "*Who? The trainer or the seal?*"

"*The trainer of course. Where would a seal keep her money?*" Bernice asked. She had such a dignified manner that it was sometimes hard to tell when she was joking. This was one of those times when I thought I ought to laugh and yet was afraid to.

She leaned over close to me so that no one else could hear. "*Anyway, seals don't care about money. All they want is top billing.*" She said it just as seriously as if she had informed me that seals ate fish.

Deciding that it was safe, I chuckled. "*I'm glad you're my friend.*"

She flashed a brief smile at me. "*And I'm glad you're mine. Do you want to work on homework sometime during vacation?*" she asked. We had some assignments due when we got back from Christmas vacation.

Treasure what you have, I told myself. Bernice was a good friend and should not be taken for granted. "*Yes, I'd like that.*"

When I went to our first class, Victoria was already at her desk. *"You really must come over and visit us now that we're neighbors."*

"I would like that," I said. But somehow even a visit with the Barringtons did not seem very important now that Papa was sick. Besides, I figured Ann was bound to be wherever Victoria was, and I wasn't sure if I had the stomach for that much of Ann.

"I really mean it," she said, and then lowered her voice. *"It would be nice to have someone to talk to."*

I shook my head sardonically. *"You have Ann and the others."*

"Yes, but they're so— " She bit her lip as she caught herself.

I tried to explain the situation gently. *"Ann wouldn't approve if you had me over."*

"Ah," she sighed, and her shoulders sagged sadly.

I realized she didn't have a choice.

I thought about some of the odd things I'd seen earlier—like their moving their own things rather than hiring someone. They must have had money before, but maybe they didn't now. Mama had been the first to pick up on it when she'd noticed the frayed shirt cuff. I had no idea how expensive watercress was in winter. But I bet it couldn't cost too much. Maybe her father had wasted their food money on the orange. So perhaps she had to eat the watercress sandwiches just as we had once had to eat lettuce sandwiches—because it was all we could afford.

Even more importantly, that explained why Mr. Barrington had been so eager to court Ann. He needed the job her father gave him. And he had used Victoria as the bait. And the story about understanding his family history was just an attempt to save face.

In a way this was all Victoria's fault. After all, if she didn't ask for things like oranges and other fancy goods, her father could save more money. She shouldn't let him spoil her this way.

Suddenly I realized that I was thinking like Mama, but Victoria looked so dejected that I couldn't scold her.

"*When he's found out everything he wants to know about his family, he can quit, because it won't matter what Ann thinks*," I whispered.

"*I hope it's soon*," Victoria sighed. "*He's so miserable.*"

As I stared at Victoria, I thought about my own father. His life would be so much easier if he could stand at a bank counter. Instead, he worked sixteen hours or more some days. Sometimes after he'd washed the clothes in boiling water, his scholar's hands seemed like lobster claws. And I felt even guiltier for the things I had thought about Papa.

At lunchtime Ann and her flock were preening on a bench as usual. "*I was thinking of cutting my hair*," one of the flock was saying. She was a tall, particularly silly girl called Maude. "*What do you think, Ann?*"

Ann was in her element. She toyed with her own brown sausage curls and looked at Victoria, sitting next to her. "*I was thinking of doing the same thing myself. I'm getting tired of looking old-fashioned.*" I guess that now that Victoria Barrington was acceptable, so was her hairstyle.

Victoria started to rise when she saw me pass by with Bernice and Florie. *"Oh, Joan."*

However, Ann was not about to let her go. Grabbing Victoria's wrist, Ann said, *"Victoria, what would you advise Maude?"*

Victoria gave me a frustrated, helpless look and sat back down.

I suppose for the sake of my father's job, I could have been nice to Ann. But I doubt if I could have pretended to be part of Ann's flock, because that meant behaving just like Ann, dressing like Ann, thinking like Ann. Poor Victoria would have to forget about an awful lot that made her special.

And though I didn't have the right, I thought I ought to offer her the chance to get away for a little while. *"Would you like to eat with us when you're done advising Maude?"*

Ann beckoned to Victoria like someone twitching at the leash of her pet dog. *"Quit pestering her, Joan. I think Victoria has bent over backward trying to be nice to you because she's polite."*

"It's up to you, Victoria," I said.

Victoria hesitated, and for one moment I thought she might act for herself. She would be all right if she could give herself a small period to separate herself from the flock and not let Ann control her.

I found myself wishing her to walk away. It didn't have to be with me. She could go off by herself, if only for a few minutes. "Don't let yourself be sold," I wished silently. And for a moment her body tensed, as if she were going to rise and escape.

Perhaps she thought of her father then. With a hopeless little shrug to me, she remained where she was. *"No thank you, Joan."*

Ann took her hand, smiling smugly at me. *"So do tell us what Maude should do."*

No more discussion of poems or chambers of flowers or jasmine tea. Victoria's eyes looked frustrated and sad. And I thought that a bird's eyes must look just the same way when its wings were being clipped to keep it on the ground.

"Victoria." Ann's voice grew more preemptory.

Mr. Barrington might clerk in the bank, but it was really Victoria who was going to pay the bills. *"I'm sorry,"* I blurted out.

As a silent acknowledgment, Victoria twisted one corner of her mouth into a tired, wry smile.

Ann misinterpreted my apology. *"And you should be. Victoria's been very understanding, but you've mistaken patience for interest. She really isn't your kind. Do run along and don't be quite so tiresome, Joan."*

"Who is my kind?" Victoria wondered out loud.

"Why . . . your friends, dear," Ann said, motioning to her flock.

Victoria seemed to reach some decision. Reluctantly she turned her back on me to focus on Ann and her flock. *"Short hair is easier to take care of,"* she informed Maude.

Would I have been willing to make that kind of sacrifice for my own father? I didn't think I could, so I decided not to judge Victoria. I would just feel sorry for her.

As Bernice, Florie and I headed for a bench where Henrietta and Havana sat, I couldn't help thinking that I'd been dead wrong about Mr. Barrington. All this time I'd thought he was the ideal father. Well, I couldn't blame him for trying to feed himself and Victoria. It was his methods I might question. He'd as good as sold his daughter to find employment.

Henrietta and Havana were glad to make room for us. And as Bernice sat down, she mused, *"I told you that Victoria has the eyes of an actress."*

Florie sighed. *"I wouldn't mind having the eyes of Theda Bara. Such expression."* Theda Bara was a popular movie star who looked like she laid on eyeliner with a trowel.

Bernice shook her head. *"That's not what I meant. Victoria is always watching her audience. I do not think she means everything she says."*

"Don't be jealous," Henrietta whispered earnestly. *"It doesn't become you."*

"I'm just describing what I see," Bernice said stiffly, but she did not say anything more.

After lunch none of the students paid much attention to the lessons—not with vacation beginning tomorrow and Christmas looming a week later. Even the teachers seemed distracted.

As soon as school was over, "Merry Christmas" echoed and re-echoed everywhere as the excited students said their good-byes and a couple of impromptu snowball fights began.

I fell in with Havana and Bernice as they moved

outside. "*Will you be at choir practice tomorrow, Joan?*" Bernice asked.

I didn't have a particularly good voice, but I enjoyed being with my friends. "*Yes, I'll see you then.*" I stopped at the street corner to wait for Bobby and Emily.

"*Later then,*" Havana said, and waved.

As I stood there, Ann and her flock twittered by. All of them were eagerly discussing going to Ann's holiday party. They didn't notice Victoria walking a step behind them. She glanced at them and then paused as the group went on.

"No *lift today?*" I asked.

"*Father's already hard at work,*" Victoria said.

"*Of course,*" I said, feeling embarrassed. "*I should have guessed.*"

She hesitated as if wanting to explain more. "*Things don't always work out as we would like.*"

"*Victoria.*" Ann's voice floated clear and imperious through the various conversations on the street. "*We need your advice on the napkin holders.*" She gave a little hop in the snow. "*Oh, and then perhaps your father can help us shop for them.*"

"*He's working in the bank,*" Victoria reminded her with thin patience.

Ann waved a hand airily. "*I'll have a talk with Father.*"

Apparently Mr. Barrington was not only going to be the Woods' bank clerk but Ann's personal chauffeur as well.

With a resigned little sigh Victoria took a step away. "*I have to be going.*"

"*Good luck,*" I said, and watched her hurry through the slush to Ann. As she and Victoria started off again, the flock closed round them, hiding them from sight.

I realized then that there were far worse duties than having to learn Chinese and work in a laundry. One was having to be nice to Ann.

fifteen

I was surprised and frightened that for once there was no interrogation today. When I burst through the laundry door, it was only Mama at the counter. She had a ledger book spread open on the countertop, but when she raised her head, I saw her worried expression.

"Where's Papa?" I asked Mama.

She gave me a warning look as Bobby and Emily followed me into the laundry. "Papa's in bed," she announced for their sake. "He has a stomachache."

"It's not the influenza, is it?" Bobby asked. A few years ago there had been bad epidemics of influenza that had killed many people. Uncle Bing had lost a son.

"No, it's not the influenza," Mama said, patting him reassuringly on the head.

"Did you ask Miss Lucy to get a doctor?" I asked.

"No. He wouldn't let me. He won't see any doctor she recommends." She went back to her ledger book as if the numbers could distract her from her real anxiety.

I looked at Mama. She looked terribly tired, and suddenly I knew what I had to do.

Emily tugged at my sleeve. "Will Papa be all right, Joan?" she asked.

I forced myself to smile. "Yes, but I think we have to forget about Christmas. We don't want to upset him any more."

Bobby folded his arms. "I guess it can wait another year."

I thought I might have to argue with Emily, but she nodded too. "It'll be even better then."

Mama looked up in surprise. "You're good children," she said gratefully.

Coming from Mama, that was high praise. "Will Miss Lucy understand?" I wondered.

"Papa already said no," Mama said.

"I don't think she believed him, though," I said.

Mama fell back on her old habits. "You're good at explaining these things to people."

I stuffed down any resentment. This was no time to start another fight. "All right."

With heavy steps I went out the kitchen to the little courtyard. The fairy light in the window was glowing like a small bit of frozen flame. Lovely Christmas carols were coming faintly from Miss Lucy's house, played on what sounded like chimes. If elves made Christmas music, this is exactly how it would have sounded.

Even if I had not had an errand, the sound would have drawn me. When I knocked at the door, Miss Lucy opened it instantly. She had an apron over her clothes, and a lock of hair had strayed down and stuck to her perspiring forehead. Miss Lucy was a wonderful cook who loved to fill people with food, and I think she had her happiest moments in her kitchen.

When she opened her door, the heavenly Christmas music poured from her house, filling the whole courtyard. Miss Lucy seemed as lively as her Christmas music, so I felt like I was about to pluck the wings from a cherub.

"*Oh, Joan. How is your father?*" she asked.

"*He's lying down,*" I said.

"*Is he well enough for me to talk to him? I'm sure I can change his mind about Christmas.*" Behind her, I saw, the kitchen table was full of bowls with popcorn and cranberries.

"*What are all those for?*" I asked.

"*As soon as I talk to your father, we can string our decorations,*" she said. Though Miss Lucy was as sweet as could be, it was a mistake to think she couldn't be stubborn. "*Are Emily and Bobby back yet? If all of us work together, we might just make it by Christmas. We're going to have such fun this year.*"

Miss Lucy wanted Christmas so badly that she just wouldn't take "no" for an answer.

I felt like such a failure. I had not only let down Papa as a daughter, but I had let down Miss Lucy as a friend. It was a moment before I could get the bad news out. "*Miss Lucy, I'm afraid there's not going to be any Christmas this year.*"

She flapped a hand at me. "*Fiddlesticks—there's*

always Christmas. Your father's bellyache made him contrary the other day." She wasn't about to give up on reviving her happy memories.

Her dream was as fragile and delicate as one of her imported glass ornaments, and I felt as if she had entrusted it to me and I was about to smash it on the ground. *"With Papa being sick, we think it'll be too much commotion for him,"* I tried to explain.

"Oh," Miss Lucy said. *"Emily was so counting on Christmas."*

So was Miss Lucy—from the agitated way she clutched her hands together.

"Emily understands now though," I said. I hoped Miss Lucy would too.

She shook her head. *"How could your father disappoint her like that? Doesn't he care?"*

"He cares," I said, trying to defend him. *"He made all these sacrifices to come to America and then bring Mama over. And now he works such long hours that he hardly ever sleeps."* As I spoke, I realized it was true: Papa did love us.

He might not have Mr. Barrington's fancy clothes and words, but he was a far better father. Papa never would have "sold" me for a job. Suddenly I knew who was the true gentleman.

"My father doesn't show his love in all the ways American parents might," I explained. *"You can't just judge him on the basis of one holiday."*

Miss Lucy patted my shoulder. *"It speaks well of you to forgive him."*

"There's nothing to forgive," I said—and meant it.

Miss Lucy looked so sad that I thought I should say more, but I didn't know what.

When the song slowed and stopped, she didn't even notice. I thought I might distract her. She loved showing us her family's things. Besides, I was also curious about the source of the heavenly song. *"What was making the Christmas music?"*

Miss Lucy roused herself. *"I dug out Grandfather's music box. It's so much nicer than one of those horrid phonographs."*

"I've heard music boxes before, and they never sounded like that," I said.

"They were probably small ones," Miss Lucy explained. *"Do you have a moment?"*

I really should have gone home to help Mama, but I couldn't resist. At my nod she led me back into the parlor, which was still piled with all her Christmas things. She had cleared a space on the edge of the table for a huge polished wooden box. Inlaid wood formed a design of wooded hills on the sides. *"Grandfather loved Christmas music."* Inside the box was a large metal disk covered with little holes. She took it from the box and selected another one from a stack of dusty disks. Placing the old one to the side, she picked up a clean cotton rag and wiped the new disk. On its silvery surfaces our shapes appeared in mottled colors. *"After he died, I never felt like playing them, so it's wonderful to have an excuse to get them out now."*

Setting the disk inside the box, she turned a crank to wind it up, and the music started again. The large metal disk rotated inside, filling the house with full, sonorous music. And for a moment I felt like a window for Christmas sunlight.

Suddenly we heard the screech of brakes outside, and then Mr. Barrington's horn started to honk angrily. *"I hope poor James is all right."* Throwing down the cloth, Miss Lucy ran out of the parlor, down the hallway and straight out her kitchen door, still in just her dress and apron.

I grabbed the old coat from its hook by the door and followed her. *"Miss Lucy, your coat. It's cold."*

Miss Lucy, though, hurried down the alley, heedless of snow or ice. When we reached Main Street, we saw that Mr. Barrington's car had stopped in the middle of the street. Harold had improvised a barricade by swinging his garage truck across both lanes.

When Miss Lucy came to a startled halt, I draped the coat about her shoulders.

Mr. Barrington tooted his horn angrily. *"Do you mind getting out of the way, my good man?"* Victoria and Ann were next to him on the front seat while a pile of packages sat in the back.

Harold leaned his head back insolently. *"I ain't your man, and I ain't very good when you come down to it."* Picking up a big wrench, he climbed out of his truck. *"You been dodging me all day, but you ain't getting away this time."* He reached inside his coverall and pulled out a slip of paper. *"I don't want any scrap of paper from a fancy Pittsburgh bank. I want cold, hard cash. I stayed up all night to fix your dent. Now you pay me."*

Mr. Barrington waved his hand nervously as a small

crowd began to gather. "*We'll discuss the matter tomorrow.*"

Ann was dying of mortification in the front seat. "*How dare you talk to Mr. Barrington like that? Get out of the way!*"

However, Harold stroked the fender of the car. "*A piece of fine-tuned machinery like this needs a lot of maintenance. I figure if you was in Pittsburgh long enough to open a checking account, your car would have needed some work on it. A mechanic don't get to work too often on a fancy car like this. You remember working on it. So I called around. Ain't nobody in Pittsburgh heard of you.*"

Mr. Barrington did something with the clutch, and his car began to back up.

"*Stop right there.*" Harold leaped forward and slammed the wrench on top of the wheel. Mr. Barrington stopped. "*I'm holding on to this car until I get my money.*"

Mr. Barrington looked at him coldly. "*You can't do that.*"

Harold waved the wrench. "*This is the only lawyer I need. Now get out of that car.*"

Harold wasn't prepared when Mr. Barrington opened his car door suddenly. It hit him so hard that he dropped the wrench and fell over backward. Immediately, Mr. Barrington backed his car up again.

"*Father, stop! We have to see how badly hurt he is,*" Victoria said.

"*That ruffian has done far more damage to our good*

name than any dent I could give to his skull," Mr. Barrington declared but he stopped.

Panicking, Ann tried to get away. *"Let me out."*

Harried, Mr. Barrington snapped, *"It's all a misunderstanding. Please calm down."*

Ann was almost in tears. *"I want to get out now,"* she said frantically.

Several people from the crowd ran into the snowy street to form human barricades so he could not move forward or backward.

"What's going on here?" Sheriff Eustace boomed. The sheriff, a heavyset man with flakes of piecrust in his beard, strolled up to us. On his head he wore a derby, and his thick frame threatened to burst out of his black wool overcoat.

Mr. Barrington pointed. *"That ruffian tried to intimidate me, so naturally I answered the threat."*

Ann jumped out. *"I want to go home."*

"Jack, get Harold's truck out of the way," the sheriff called to a young man in the crowd.

Unbuttoning his raccoon coat so he could climb into the truck, Jack got into the cab. *"Right, sheriff."*

In the meantime Eustace walked over to Harold, who was sitting up with a groan. *"I told you that this"*—the sheriff picked up the wrench and pitched it into the gutter—*"was no substitute for a law degree. Can you stand?"*

When Harold nodded his head, he winced. *"Yeah, Eustace."*

Eustace helped him to his feet. *"Come on then. We'll*

go down to my office and get this straightened out."

As Jack parked the truck at the curb, Eustace started to take the packages from the backseat of Mr. Barrington's car.

"Those are mine!" Ann shrilled.

Eustace was used to dealing with the Woods. *"And here they are."* He began to stack them at Ann's feet. *"Jack, would you use Harold's truck to drive Miss Wood home?"*

Jack paused with his leg out of the truck cab. *"You bet,"* he said, and winked at Ann.

Ann looked like she would rather have ridden in an oxcart than ride with Jack. *"Don't bend the packages."*

"We'll get you home," Jack promised as he jumped out. He didn't take his eyes off Ann as she climbed into the truck. Hastily then he transferred the remaining packages from the backseat of Mr. Barrington's car and tossed them into the back of the truck. Then he flung in the ones on the sidewalk.

Running around to the driver's side, he pulled himself behind the wheel. *"My name's Jack,"* he said to Ann.

"Yes, I heard." Ann's lips were pressed together so tightly that they were a thin, bloodless line, and she tried to look in any direction but Jack's.

The truck backfired once, causing the whole crowd to cough. As it pulled away, we could hear Jack chattering away at the silent, angry Ann.

Now that he had safely disposed of Ann, Eustace started to guide Harold to the backseat of Mr. Barrington's car. *"You just lie down back here."*

Mr. Barrington objected. *"He's covered with grease,*

and that's genuine cordovan leather."

"My wife has a recipe that'll take the grease out of anything," Eustace assured him and opened the rear door. *"I'll get it when we sort things out at the jail."*

We could still hear Mr. Barrington objecting as they drove off. Once the car was out of sight, the crowd began to break up. When they left, we saw only Victoria standing forlornly.

"Victoria," I said.

Victoria, though, didn't speak to me. Instead she raised her chin bravely and turned to Miss Lucy. *"Miss Bradshaw, could I speak to you in private?"*

"Of course, my dear," Miss Lucy said, holding the coat collar tight around her throat so it wouldn't fall off.

They walked back along the alley, their heads bent together.

sixteen

That afternoon and night Mr. Barrington was all Bobby and Emily could talk about. I didn't see any sign of Victoria. But while I felt sorry for her, I was more concerned with Papa. His illness seemed far worse than any troubles with Harold.

I wanted to tell Papa how sorry I was and that I loved him and knew now that he loved me. I just hoped it wasn't too late.

I went to bed early—partly to get away from Bobby and Emily—but I didn't sleep well. And I woke when I heard the thump outside.

Careful not to wake Emily, who slept by the window, I looked out. In the light of the streetlamp, the snow glistened just like a Christmas card. On the sidewalk, Mr. Barrington was struggling to lift a trunk into the back of his automobile while Victoria tried to pull it from the other side.

Curious, I eased out of bed. Then, picking up my shoes, I padded across the cold floor toward the door.

"*Toboggan,*" Emily mumbled.

I froze, but when she didn't say anything, I looked over my shoulder. She was still asleep.

Tiptoeing to the door, I opened it, cringing as the hinges squeaked. One day I was going to have to oil them. I glanced back at Emily, but I had not woken her up.

The laundry was silent and dark as I walked quietly down the hallway and down the steps. When I was at the foot of the stairs, I pulled on my shoes, not bothering to tie them up.

Taking my coat from a hook, I went out the kitchen door. The snow crunched under my shoes as I hurried through the courtyard and down the alley.

By the time I reached the sidewalk, the Barringtons had already secured the last trunk to the automobile, and Victoria was struggling to push the car onto the street while Mr. Barrington steered.

"*Victoria, what are you doing?*" I called softly.

Victoria's head snapped up guiltily, and she whirled around. "*Joan.*"

Mr. Barrington leaned out from the driver's side. "*Oh, hello,*" he said sheepishly. "*I regret that family matters urgently require our leaving town. The car's so powerful, it's rather noisy. I was afraid that if I started it up too close to you, we'd wake you up. I already imposed enough when we moved in.*"

He probably could have charmed me into believing him before his run-in with Harold, but not anymore.

"*What about Miss Lucy?*" I demanded.

Mr. Barrington looked hurt. "*You wound me to the quick, child. We've left payment for her in the cottage.*"

"*Why don't you leave it with me instead?*" I said suspiciously. "*I'll make sure she gets it.*"

"*We couldn't trouble you, my dear.*" The recent embarrassing scene in the street hadn't affected Mr. Barrington's charm. "*We've known you only a little while, but we consider you a good friend. So the saddest part of our departure is having to leave you. But we'll write as soon as we have a new address.*"

I started to walk back toward the house. "*I'd better wake Miss Lucy.*"

Victoria stopped me. "*We were there only a few days,*" she reasoned.

So they hadn't left the money. Mr. Barrington was worse than a snob. He was a thief. "*Even so, Miss Lucy's my friend. I can't let you cheat her. And is there anyone else besides her and Harold you owe money to?*"

Victoria spoke hastily. "*I know what you think of us, but you're wrong. My father's one fault is that he was once too trusting. Father listened to an old college chum and lost everything.*"

"*Now, Victoria,*" Mr. Barrington scolded his daughter quietly, "*it wasn't Morgan's fault. I should have known better than to listen to a man whose sole distinction in college was that he could recite the Greek alphabet backward in just one breath.*"

Victoria rolled her eyes and looked at me as if to say: See what I have to deal with?

I didn't know what to believe anymore. "*Were you really in Europe?*" I asked.

"*Of course,*" Mr. Barrington said indignantly. "*Our photographs are in one of these trunks.*" He craned his neck as if trying to figure out which one had the proof.

Victoria stroked the furred collar of her coat. "*Father tried to protect me as long as he could—when he really didn't have to. I would have understood if we had had to live on a smaller scale, but he was afraid to disappoint me. I still can't get him to stop—like with the orange.*" Her eyes pleaded silently with me to understand.

I realized she felt responsible now for the sad state of their finances. This was the other side of having every wish fulfilled by your father. In a way he was like a machine that kept trying to spew out gifts. "*It's not your fault,*" I tried to reassure her.

"*You were raised to be a Barrington. You had the right to certain expectations,*" Mr. Barrington insisted.

"*I'm not entirely innocent either.*" She smiled weakly.

What had Bernice said about her? Eyes of an actress. Was there anything about her or her father that wasn't fake?

If I let them go, it would be like stealing money from Miss Lucy's pocket myself, but all I could think of was Victoria standing so lonely upon the street corner while Eustace took her father away.

No matter what choice I made, it would be a bad one. Either decision seemed equally wrong and equally right. Wake Miss Lucy or let Victoria leave with her father?

"*Please, Joan,*" Victoria said.

I tried to offer her a way out. *"Miss Lucy would help. We all would,"* I said.

Victoria nodded toward the automobile. *"You know my father by now. Can you see him behind bars?"*

"Don't exaggerate, dear," Mr. Barrington said. *"It's really all a misunderstanding with Harold and the others."*

In how many cities in Europe and America had people "misunderstood" Mr. Barrington? It wouldn't have surprised me if he had sweet-talked his way across two continents, leaving Victoria to pick up the pieces.

I realized now that I had been mistaken about the Barringtons. Mr. Barrington wasn't taking care of Victoria; Victoria was taking care of him.

Often my parents made me feel as if we had switched roles whenever we had to deal with Americans. As the translator and cultural interpreter, I wound up acting like the adult and they like children. And Victoria did the same thing in her own way. Despite her expensive clothes and her travels around the world, we were sisters.

I wondered if my eyes looked like Victoria's, sad and knowing—the old woman's eyes in the young girl's face.

"I wish . . ." Victoria began to say but her voice faltered.

"What?" I asked.

"Nothing," she mumbled, embarrassed.

What had she tried to wish for? That she could stay? That we could have become better friends?

I wished it too. Beyond race and class, we were two of a kind. It was sad to meet a twin only to lose her.

"You'll never move this automobile by yourselves," I said to Victoria.

"There's no other choice," she said, setting her shoulder against the rear again.

"You'll need help," I said. Taking up a position next to her, I dug my shoes into the snow and leaned against their automobile too. At first I thought it was frozen to the street, but then slowly it began to move.

While Mr. Barrington steered, we pushed it down the street. The compact snow made little grunting noises beneath our shoes, and for a moment there was no sound except the panting of our breaths. With each yard the automobile picked up speed; and with each yard I felt sadder and sadder.

Finally Mr. Barrington called, *"That's enough, ladies. Stand back."*

The automobile rolled a few more yards forward under its own momentum, and then he started it up. The powerful engine roared into life, echoing in the cold, dark street.

We straightened up, puffing from our efforts, while the automobile continued on for another ten feet and then stopped. Mr. Barrington cheerfully poked his head out the window. *"Time to go."*

I turned to Victoria. *"We've known one another only a short time, but I'll miss you."*

"I'll miss you too," she said, hugging me fiercely. And then, just as suddenly, she had let me go and was running around the automobile to the passenger side.

As I heard the door shut, I ran a few steps farther into the street. *"Good-bye,"* I called softly.

Victoria, though, didn't answer. She didn't even look back.

"Tallyho!" Mr. Barrington said as he released the brake. The powerful automobile leaped forward like a hound whose leash has just been dropped. As it raced down the street, the window on the passenger side was frantically rolled down. Victoria extended a hand and waved a farewell. Idly I noticed that her glove was kid leather and dyed to match her coat.

What a strange life to have to lead: to watch over a father who was a perpetual boy. With a guilty twinge I thought of my own father lying sick upstairs in the laundry. For all his shortcomings, he always shouldered more than his share of the work.

A white dot drifted back and forth lazily under the streetlight. And then a second and a third, floating down like tiny pale leaves. Suddenly the street was filled with snowflakes whirling about. The next moment the automobile was hidden from sight.

Poor Victoria. Did she hope they could flee forever, or did she want to stop sometimes? I thought she had really wanted to rest here. Maybe she had even dreamed that her father could earn enough to settle their debts so they could quit running. That's why she had been willing to put up with Ann. When would Victoria finally feel like she had paid back her father? Probably never.

Snowflakes brushed my cheeks. I heard them melting and dying against my ears with soft sounds. Suddenly I realized that my body was shivering, and I turned back to the alley.

Once inside the laundry again, I took off my shoes and wiped them carefully. Hanging up my coat, I tiptoed back up the stairs with my shoes in one hand.

By the time I returned them to their old place in my room, my feet were like ice. So I was glad to crawl back under the quilt.

I had barely put my head on my pillow again when Emily muttered *"Toboggan"* again. Then she rolled next to me. After being outside in the cold, I felt as if her little body gave off enough heat to be a furnace. I snuggled against her, glad of the company.

seventeen 

The next morning Papa was even sicker. He wasn't eating anything anymore, and all he drank was warm milk.

Of course, there was no hiding it from Bobby and Emily now. As we stood beside Papa's bed, we stared at the quiet figure in the bed. It didn't seem like our father at all. He was so weak.

I spoke softly so I wouldn't wake him. "Mama, I know Papa didn't want an American doctor, but we need to get one. I don't think there's time to find a Chinese doctor and bring him to Clarksburg."

Mama sat in a chair while she clasped Papa's hand. With her free hand she stroked his cheek, but he did not stir. "Go ask Miss Lucy to recommend one."

Putting on my coat, I went out into the courtyard. But Miss Lucy didn't answer her door no matter how loudly

I knocked. Finally I saw her come out of the cottage. She was usually so energetic, but today she dragged her feet like she was a hundred years old.

"Did you want something, Joan?" she asked wearily.

I went over to her. *"Miss Lucy, what's wrong?"*

"The Barringtons are gone." She shook her head. *"Not only did I bail him out, but I lent him the money to settle his bill with Harold. And then there was his hotel bill too. They explained it was all a misunderstanding, because their funds were being transferred from Paris."*

So the Barringtons had cheated Miss Lucy out of more than a few days' rent. It made me feel even worse about last night. *"They could sweet-talk birds from a tree,"* I said.

She fussed with her shawl. *"If it was just him, I would chalk it up to his being a young rogue and my being a foolish old woman. But it was Victoria too. She made me feel so sorry for her, what with her father about to go to jail and all. And in the spirit of Christmas, I thought I'd help her out. She promised to pay me back right away, as soon as they received their money from Paris, but she was just flimflamming me. The child's as bad as her father, and that's what really hurts."*

I thought of what Victoria had said last night and got mad. No, she wasn't "entirely innocent." She was a thief and a liar, and I had helped her. I felt mad at her and even madder at myself for helping them.

"I'm s-so sorry," I stammered guiltily. *"I caught them leaving, and I let them go. But I didn't realize how much they owed you."*

"Then they fooled us both." Miss Lucy paused by her door. *"All they left was dust."* She caught herself. *"No, I guess the dust was already there."*

"I'll do chores to work off the money," I offered.

She gave me an affectionate peck on the cheek. *"Don't blame yourself. It's no shame to be charitable. Blame them for exploiting that."*

I felt like a sack of cement had just been lifted off my shoulders. *"It's a wonder how they could pack and move so quietly,"* I said. *"When they moved in, it was so noisy."*

"They've probably had a lot of practice," Miss Lucy said ruefully. *"But you came to see me about something, Joan?"*

I felt funny asking for a favor after helping to cheat her. *"Could you recommend a doctor?"*

She went from worrying about the Barringtons to worrying about Papa. *"Here I am fretting about money when there's a friend sick. What kind of miserable Christian am I?"*

All she cared about was helping now. Tapping a finger against her lips, she thought awhile and then gave a nod. *"Josh was a nail biter when he was a little boy in my class, but he knows his medicine."*

She seemed to have recovered her old energy as I followed her into the kitchen, where a telephone hung on the wall. Though I had seen her place calls before, I still hadn't tired of watching. Picking up the conelike receiver, she held it to her hear while she wound the crank on the side vigorously. When the operator came on, she had to stand almost on tiptoe to speak into the separate mouthpiece. *"Polly, will you get me Dr. Josh?"*

When Dr. Josh Hawkins arrived, he proved to be a solid little man with a derby hat and long black coat that hung past his knees. His black bag looked worn from hard use.

After a thorough examination, he took Miss Lucy, Mama, and me out into the hallway. And with a shake of his head he confessed that though he could give Papa something for the pain, he could provide no definite diagnosis.

Mama's English was good enough for everyday conversation, but she had trouble with more complicated words, so I explained.

"Oh," Mama said in a small voice. With both hands, she clutched the bottle of pills the doctor had given her. She looked terribly small for all her burdens.

Miss Lucy planted her fists on her hips. *"My grandfather would have said 'twaddle,' Josh."*

His professional dignity wounded, the doctor fidgeted with the snap on his black bag. *"Miss Bradshaw, your grandfather would have given you the identical diagnosis."*

Miss Lucy reared back as if he had just insulted her family's honor. *"I'll go through his old medical journals myself."*

"You kept them?" Josh asked in amazement.

Miss Lucy shrugged. *"We Bradshaws never throw away a book. A book that comes into this house never leaves, but I was referring to the journals he kept about his patients. There's more wisdom on one page of his journals than in ten volumes of your medical books."*

"Fine, but for the record, we don't use leeches any-more," the doctor snapped.

"And do you still chew your nails?" Miss Lucy shot back.

Embarrassed, the doctor hid his free hand in his coat pocket. *"I'll be back tomorrow,"* he promised Mama, and left.

I sagged against the wall. Without Papa the laundry would be a joyless place. Mama was the serious, practical sort while Papa was the one who liked to hear laughter. Too late I had come to realize the value of my own parents.

Miss Lucy patted me on the shoulder. *"Don't worry, Joan. Your father will be all right."*

Mama, though, was as practical as ever. With a shake of her shoulders she put aside her own fears. Taking my arm, she pulled me back to my feet. "In the meantime we have a laundry to run."

The hardest part was trying to pretend to Emily and Bobby that Papa would be all right. If Bobby had any suspicions, he was old enough to keep them to himself, but Emily spewed out a fountain of questions: What? Why? How long?

I tried my best to ease her mind, but Emily was almost a professional worrywart. Though she acted as if she were tougher than Bobby, the truth was that any change in our routine upset her.

However, she didn't have much time to worry. We did our best to help Mama run the laundry, though it meant double chores for everyone. It made all of us realize just how much work Papa did.

Now that it was Christmas vacation, we worked all day. Of course, no one spoke about Christmas anymore. Even Bobby buckled down. When his friends came to get him to help build a snow fort, he refused.

Early that evening, when Florie and my other friends came to pick me up for choir practice, Mama told me to go. However, I felt I had to be at least as good as Bobby.

"I'm so sorry," Florie said. *"It's nothing serious, is it?"*

"The doctor doesn't know." I shrugged.

I received a sympathetic pat from Henrietta and even a short shoulder rub from Havana.

Bernice hugged me reassuringly. *"He will be all right. You will see."*

"I hope so," I said.

When they had left, I spent the next couple of hours folding clothes and wrapping them up in blue paper. Eventually, though, I ran out of work to do. I hated that. Even though I was exhausted from a full day's work, the lull gave me too much time to think, and whenever I thought about the past few days, I felt guiltier.

I staggered up the steps to my parents' bedroom to see if Papa wanted anything.

When I peeked in on him, he was lying asleep in his bed. His face had taken on an odd, pale, waxy look. It was as if someone had substituted a mannequin for my father. What I saw in that bed was empty of what made him Papa. Then, as I watched, he stirred and gave a groan.

"Papa," I whispered.

His eyes remained closed, as if he were still unconscious, but his face twisted into a grimace, as if someone had stuck a knife into him. It was terrible to see someone I loved in that much pain and not be able to do anything about it. Feeling helpless, I shut the door again.

Across the street the choir was practicing. I had lost track of the time. Half groggy, I went looking for Mama and found her sitting in a chair in the drying room with her face in her hands. Before I could say anything, I saw something drip from between her fingers. I realized with a start that she was crying.

I wanted to go to her and comfort her, but what could I say? That Papa would be all right? That was something we said to Bobby and Emily, but even they no longer believed it.

Mama liked to have people think she was strong. I knew she wouldn't have wanted to know that I had seen her in a moment of weakness, giving in to her fears.

As silently as I could, I tiptoed back into the hallway. Needing something to do, I thought of Miss Lucy and her medical journals. Any hope was better than no hope at all. And it would feel good to be trying to do something to help Papa. So I went across the courtyard to help her go through her grandfather's journals.

I always looked for the fairy light on her kitchen window—the sight of the light pouring through the fiery sides always cheered me up. But it wasn't there.

I found her in the parlor with dozens of old, dusty, leather-bound books spread across her table. A teapot sat in one corner, steam rising from its spout. A cup was next to it, with a plate on which rested a half-eaten cookie. The music box was thundering "Deck the Hall" from the parlor so loudly that the entire house vibrated—as if it were a music box itself.

"Is your father any better?" she asked solicitously.

"No," I said, stepping inside. *"Have you had any luck?"*

Miss Lucy reached a hand beneath her eyeglasses to pinch the bridge of her nose. *"I'm afraid not."*

I pulled a chair away from the table and picked up a journal. *"What am I looking for?"* I asked.

Miss Lucy closed the door and poured me a cup of tea. *"Any case like your father's. Symptoms like stomachache."*

As I sat down, I glanced at the empty windowsill. *"Nothing happened to your lovely fairy light, did it?"*

"Oh, that old thing," Miss Lucy said. *"I was getting tired of it."*

"But you said once that it had been your mother's," I said. I started to get a bad feeling.

"It was just gathering dust," Miss Lucy said, sitting down again.

I looked around the kitchen, noticing that other decorative little things were gone. I wondered what else I would find missing if I examined other rooms in her house. *"You didn't sell it, did you?"*

"There's too much to clean in this house," Miss Lucy said, bending her head over a journal.

"You did sell it, and it's all my fault," I said. I could

feel tears edging up in the corners of my eyes, and then the kitchen started to blur.

I felt Miss Lucy's hand on mine. *"It's all right, dear. I have too many things. Can't keep them where I'm going, so I might as well pass them on to someone who'll appreciate them."*

"I'm so sorry." When I shook my head, the tears coursed down my cheeks.

I heard Miss Lucy's chair scrape across the floor, and the next moment she was handing me a napkin. *"Stop crying, dear. You're getting the journal wet."*

I would have apologized again, but another sounded silly. So after wiping my eyes, I opened the old journal. Fine dust rose and it made my nose tickle. The old binding made a crackling noise, and the ink was turning brown with age. Miss Lucy's grandfather had written in a big, bold hand with exuberant loops.

Miss Lucy set a plate of cookies next to me, and I began to nibble them as I read. The cookies were rich and buttery, and I savored every crumb.

From what little I knew of the local geography, he seemed to have covered a wide territory. And since he had often been paid in produce and livestock rather than with money, his buggy must have resembled a mobile barnyard more than a vehicle of mercy. Several times he had received a pig, and once he had been paid with a whole cow. I hoped he hadn't had to make change.

Her grandfather had made his entries by the day rather than by the patient, so the treatment for one patient might be scattered over twenty pages or more;

and it often consisted of some old remedy whose name I didn't recognize. Sometimes there were just abbreviations that Miss Lucy didn't know.

Miss Lucy had changed the music disks five times before she concentrated on just reading. We had gone through two pots of tea and half a tin of cookies before I found an entry under "Ned." He complained of a stomachache, and from what I could make out, none of the standard cures had worked. Finally after a month, Miss Lucy's grandfather had written in exasperation, "*What's wrong!!!!!*" The exclamation points looked like a wall of spears.

Underneath it he had written another note: "*Try Jack Selden.*"

"*Do you know who Jack Selden is?*" I asked Miss Lucy.

Miss Lucy wrinkled her forehead while she tried to remember that long ago. "*I think that's Uncle Jack. He was a friend of Grandfather's who had gone to teach at the medical school at Johns Hopkins. That's a famous university.*"

So her grandfather had called in the high-powered guns. "*And who's Ned?*"

"*There were a lot of Neds,*" Miss Lucy said.

I leafed back through the journal until I found the initial entry that said where Ned lived. When I told her, Miss Lucy thought again. "*Oh, Ned was an Indian. He had a blacksmith shop over there.*"

I flipped back to my original place and began to read further. About two weeks later he had written,

"Success!!!!!! Jack was right." But there was nothing about what had worked the magic.

I went through the entire journal and then worked through it again, but I couldn't find a clue. Frustrated, I slammed the book shut, but I hadn't taken into account how brittle the book was. The spine broke, and the top cover fell off.

"I'm sorry, Miss Lucy," I said.

Miss Lucy did her best to hide the fact that she was upset. *"It's nothing that can't be mended,"* she said, picking up the split-off cover.

That was when I saw the sheet of paper that had been tucked into the endpapers. When I picked it up, I saw it was on official Johns Hopkins stationery. With growing excitement, I noticed that the signature was "Jack."

And then I let out a whoop as I began to read the letter itself, then hurried to explain my shout. *"Your grandfather's friend wrote back and said that there were certain people who lacked something in the stomach that helped digest dairy products. He says it's most common among people of the 'Asiatic race.' And he speculates that there is an anthropological theory that Indians are descended from Asians who crossed a land bridge into America. It's where the Bering Strait is now."*

"But what was the cure?" Miss Lucy said, slapping the table in her impatience.

"Doctor Selden suggested to stop drinking milk," I said, passing the letter over to her.

"Oh, dear," Miss Lucy said as she read it. When she finished, she tore off her glasses. *"I feel so terrible. I was*

the one who told your father to drink milk. Maybe I really am an awful busybody."

"*You thought you were helping him,*" I said, patting her arm.

Distressed, Miss Lucy rubbed her eyes. "*It's one thing to be a fool who throws her money away. Then I hurt only myself. But it's another thing to be a know-it-all who poisons her friends.*"

"*Do you think it's worth trying?*" I asked.

"*It certainly couldn't hurt,*" Miss Lucy said. She rapped her knuckles against her forehead. "*I'm such an idiot.*"

I was sorry to see her punishing herself so. "*Papa would be the first to say that you've been a good friend to the family.*"

Miss Lucy shook her head. "*A friend doesn't try to make you do everything her way.*" She sat back with a sigh. "*And here I was sulking over Christmas like a spoiled child. This helps put things into perspective, doesn't it?*"

I would trade a healthy Papa for a lifetime of Christmases. "*It certainly does.*" I thought of why I had wanted Christmas. It hadn't really been about the presents—though it would have been nice. The hard part in January wasn't listening to everyone compare their presents. It was feeling different. I used to worry about what our friends would think if they found out we didn't celebrate Christmas. I bet if I talked to Emily and Bobby, they would say they thought the same thing.

Miss Lucy glanced at the watch that dangled from a

chain. "*Goodness. Look at the time. I'll call Josh tonight. In the meantime you should go home before your mother starts worrying.*"

When I got up, I realized my body was stiff from sitting so long. I didn't care, though. For the first time in a while I had hope. "*Thank you,*" I said, giving Miss Lucy a hug.

She hugged me back. "*We've done a good night's work, haven't we?*"

eighteen 

The laundry was quiet when I got back and took off my coat. In fact, it was so quiet that I heard the boards creak beneath my feet, though I tried to walk slowly and lightly.

Then from across the street came Bernice's beautiful soprano. As always, it made me ache to hear such lovely notes. Her voice seemed to pierce right into my heart.

And I felt a chill. There was always some moisture that found its way out of the laundry room into the general air. It made the cold air feel clammy.

Suddenly I heard a thump from Papa's study. Carefully I twisted the doorknob to see who was there.

"Hello?" I called softly.

The shade was drawn, shutting out most of the light from the streetlamp. Even so, my nose knew the entire arrangement of the room so I went inside to search for the intruder.

From the left came the faint chemical smell of the bookshelf that was Papa's library. Papa's Chinese books were all softbound, and the paper was cheap, giving off an odd odor. Against the next wall was Papa's desk and chair. My nose could detect the perfumed scent of Papa's special black inks that clung to his brushes and inkwell.

I followed the scent of the ink to his desk. My groping hands touched the cool, smooth surface of his rice paper. It made me sad to think that he might never fill it with his lovely little poems. I had been so wrong to dismiss all his learning as "old-fashioned" and "old-country." The real trick was to know what to keep and what to forget. Until I picked that up, I had better pay attention to everything.

Most of Papa's books were paperbacks, so I was surprised to feel the hard outlines of a book.

Feeling blindly along, I found the tin of matches in its usual spot. The sulfur tickled my nose when I struck a match, and I almost sneezed. Cupping my hand around the match, I turned up the gas jet of the light and lit it.

Some books stacked carelessly on a shelf had fallen down, and I restored them to their proper place. When Papa was writing one of his poems, he sometimes forgot to be neat.

Curious about the hardback, I went to the desk and dug around. I was surprised to pull out my English textbook. Papa had painstakingly and lovingly tried to repair it. My other books were there too.

A breeze riffled the pages of one of Papa's Chinese

books. The thin rice-paper pages fluttered easily. I recognized Papa's handwriting, but this wasn't one of his poems. There were long blocks of text.

When I saw the dates, I realized Papa had been keeping a journal, but this one wasn't on medicine or the laundry. Instead, I saw a Chinese phrase that seemed to be nonsense until I read it out loud. The syllables sounded out the name of Thomas Jefferson. On another page I recognized the Pythagorean theorem written out in Chinese. These were all notes from our interrogations. Beneath one day's record, Papa had written, "Must not fall behind. Must keep up with the children."

Another note on a different page almost broke my heart. Papa had written, "Losing them."

Suddenly I realized that I had been all wrong about the purpose of the interrogations. Papa had not been testing to see if we had learned anything. He had been trying to learn through us. He had been using us as his tutors, but he had been too proud to tell us. The summaries we gave him he wrote down and then studied. I was sure if I looked around the room, I would find piles of notes that were his homemade textbooks, painstakingly compiled since I had first started school.

I felt like I had fallen into the bottom of a pit at the center of the earth. I couldn't get much lower than I already was. Poor Papa. He had only been trying to get little snippets of an American education through us. And his snotty daughter had been so resentful. I was as bad as Ann. I'd made Papa think he was losing our love and respect.

There was ink still in the inkwell. When I was small,

I used to love helping Papa make it because of the perfume. He would have me take one of his special black ink sticks and rub it against the sides of the well, mixing it with water until it was just the way he liked it. I used to be terrifically proud when he said that I was the best ink maker in America. To my chagrin, I could not remember the last time I had helped him.

Tomorrow I would clean out the well and tidy up his desk so it would be all ready for him when he got better. I made myself use *when* rather than *if*. Jack Selden just had to be right again.

A breeze blew through the open door, caressing everything in the room. A corner of the window shade rose, and the room suddenly became even brighter. There was no one else in the room.

And yet as I watched the papers ripple on the desk, I felt as if I weren't alone. I jumped when I felt something touch the back of my neck. It went about the room stirring everything up, and then it slipped away into the laundry itself.

Part of me said it was only a slight wind, but my imagination said the touch had felt like an invisible hand. And I was so sleepy that I found myself believing it. It had to be Papa.

I thought of his story again. Maybe there was something to it after all—maybe his dream soul had gotten lost. Upstairs in his bed his body seemed as vacant as an abandoned house. I glanced around the dimly lit room, trying to think of the best way to guide Papa's lost soul back to his body.

In his story the wise old woman had used the girl's

blouse. I looked around for an article of clothing, but all I saw was Papa's American hat. Though he wore it whenever he stepped outside in the winter, I didn't think he would recognize it as different from anyone else's. In fact, he was always forgetting it. The same was true of all his clothes. They were just things he put on so he would not stick out.

And then I knew what would call Papa. It was the one thing that would draw his soul back to us. Reaching across the desk, my fingers closed around the stem of one of his writing brushes. Dream soul or even ghost, Papa's hand would want to close around that familiar stem.

Clutching it in my hand, I stepped back into the hallway. "Papa," I whispered. "Papa?" I tried timidly first to my left, then to my right. Beginning at the counter in the front of the laundry, I began to make my way through the building.

"Papa?" I whispered.

I thought of all the times when I was small and I had turned to Papa. He was always ready to comfort me with a smile and a few kind words. In Papa's eyes, I could do nothing wrong. And when I was small, the reverse was true: He could do no wrong in mine.

But then I had grown up and grown away. And now Papa was so alone, so alone. "I'm sorry, Papa."

I thought of what Emily had said: that you have to believe in something first to make it happen. This was no time to do things halfheartedly. "Papa?

"Papa," I called louder. "Papa, come back."

I could feel a presence in the laundry, as if the soul were playing cat and mouse with me. Then, as I neared the kitchen, I heard a board creak. I stood stock-still but heard another board creak. In the back of my mind, I knew it was probably just the boards contracting in the cold; but my heart wanted to believe it was Papa.

I whirled around, trying to face toward the sound. "Papa? Here's your brush."

I wasn't sure what sign to look for, but I was certain he was near me. Even when his souls and body were united, he could be terribly absentminded.

I almost screamed when I felt something icy grip my ankles. I stood there paralyzed until I realized it was just a breeze from somewhere.

"Papa?" The feeling was gone now.

I followed the breeze to the kitchen. The window was open a crack. I called around the kitchen, but it felt empty. Then I had a terrible thought. What if his dream soul had slipped out the window?

The key was in the lock to the door. My free hand gave it a twist and I heard the click. The cold surrounded me as I stepped through the doorway. "Papa."

The snow scrunched under my shoes. The windows in Miss Lucy's house were dark except for a light up in her bedroom.

I called softly in the courtyard. The breeze swept some of the loose snow along like a snake writhing over the surface. Or was it something else?

I followed it down the alleyway and out to the front of the laundry.

"Papa?"

In front of me a few snowflakes floated like moths beneath the streetlamp. Across the street, the church doors were open, flooding the sidewalk with light. Choir practice must have let out. Through the snowflakes, I saw the choir members like shadows as they trudged toward home.

I jumped when I heard a tree branch creak overhead and bits of snow fell, pattering on the snow on the ground. Caught between fear and hope, I looked up, but there was only an owl staring down. The white feathers around its yellow eyes made them seem as large and luminous as twin moons.

Papa's dream soul might be wandering anywhere in that cold, cold world. I couldn't see the moon or stars, just a dark-gray sheet of clouds that the stark branches clawed at.

"Papa?" I called out. I didn't want him lost. From the corner of my eye I caught sight of something moving. I whirled, but it was only the wind blowing the snow along. And yet something made me feel as if his confused dream soul were close.

"Papa?" Snow began to fall in little white dots, and the wind made swirls and eddies as if there were dozens of lost souls out that night.

"Papa." I held up the brush and felt snowflakes melt on my wrist like small, damp kisses.

Then, to my dismay, I saw some of my classmates come out of the church. There were still a few people who must have dawdled. In a moment they would be spilling into the street, hopelessly confusing Papa even more.

I felt positive that I had almost caught his dream soul. "Papa," I called urgently. The cold had crept through my dress, but I tried to ignore the chill.

Henrietta turned to stare at me. The irony flashed through my mind. I had once been so worried about fitting in that I had made my father sick over Christmas. And now I didn't care what the others thought as long as he got well. "Papa," I shouted. I could hear the folk talking to each other on the steps.

"She's gone crazy," Henrietta said.

Well, I couldn't blame her. My hair was all tangled and must have been covered with snow, and I was standing in the cold in only a dress. So much for watching my reputation. But I didn't care. At the moment all I knew was that I loved Papa so much that I ached inside.

Bernice burst down the steps and ran through the snow toward me. Tall, gawky Havana was close at her heels, and Henrietta and Florie followed on their shorter legs.

"Joan, what is wrong?" Bernice asked in her perfect pronunciation.

"My father's sick because he's lost one of his souls. I have to call it back." There wasn't time to explain more. I had to catch it. "Papa."

Henrietta backed up a step. *"Watch out. I think she's mad."*

"No, it's some kind of Chinese custom," Bernice explained.

"What custom?" Henrietta demanded.

Bernice looked at me for further elaboration, but I had to concentrate on the task at hand. "Papa," I called.

Havana tried to put a hand on my shoulder, but I shook her off. *"She's just upset."*

"You have a cup of tea when you're upset. That's crazy," Henrietta declared.

I had begun to shiver in the cold. "Papa."

"If you cannot understand it as a Chinese custom, then at least consider the fact that her nerves have been under a great strain," Bernice explained. *"And people suffering from that complaint sometimes do things to relieve the stress."*

"Like my uncle in the Great War," Florie said. *"He's still high-strung. Any high-pitched sound makes him think artillery shells are falling. Sometimes he even screams."*

"Exactly my point," Bernice said.

I tried to tell them that I wasn't doing anything odd. But I was so cold now that I could barely get it out of my chattering teeth.

Henrietta edged away from me. *"Maybe we should get help."*

"I can remember a time you had an invisible playmate," Florie said with what appeared to be an innocent smile. *"Maybe we should have gotten help for you then."*

"That was different," Henrietta protested. *"I was just pretending."*

"I remember when you thought our kindergarten teacher had sat on your playmate," Havana chimed in with the same sweet tone as Florie. *"You kicked her."*

"That was a long time ago," Henrietta said weakly.

"We all do things," Havana said. *"So no one should throw stones."*

Since people sometimes looked down at her because of her theatrical background, Bernice was more sensitive than most about her reputation. And yet when she saw how cold and helpless I was, she tried to help me by calling out loud. *"Mr. Lee."* I blessed her for that.

"Mr. Lee." That was Havana.

Florie took up the call. And finally even Henrietta. No matter how crazy it might seem, we were friends after all. Their trust and love were better than any Christmas present.

Suddenly Miss Lucy was coming toward us. *"Joan, come inside,"* she said. She was wearing just a robe and shawl. *"I spoke to Josh. He'll be here the first thing in the morning."*

I only half heard her, though. I knew what I had in my hand was the real answer. "Papa?" I called. Suddenly I felt the brush tingle against my palm—as if I had touched a wire with a small electric current going through it. I couldn't be sure, but perhaps this was the sign I had been waiting for.

"Excuse me," I said through chattering teeth. *"I have to get home."*

Miss Lucy spread her large shawl protectively over my shoulders like a hen spreading her wing for a chick. *"Come with me, dear."*

Suddenly Bernice had taken my elbow to give me support, while the others went ahead, acting as guides. *"Careful,"* Henrietta warned. *"I think the curb begins here under the snow."* She pointed to a spot in the snowbank.

I realized that it had been silly to worry about what my friends thought—whether it was Christmas or this. They were my friends and accepted me for what I was.

"Thank you," I said to them.

With Miss Lucy on one side and Bernice on the other, I began to slog along. The snow was falling harder now. Big snowflakes were hanging from the brush's bristles.

Florie had run on ahead to bang on the laundry door, but Havana pointed at the darkened windows. *"No, Mrs. Lee will be in the back."*

Henrietta high-stepped past them down the alley. *"Mrs. Lee,"* she called to Mama.

I had quite a convoy who brought me to our kitchen. Mama was standing puzzled by the door. "I came to the kitchen to make some tea and found the door open. Where were you?"

The commotion had brought Bobby and Emily. Emily was standing there in her nightgown rubbing her eyes sleepily. "Where were you?"

"No time," I blurted out. I broke away from Bernice and Miss Lucy and rushed past my family.

"Wipe your feet first," Mama called after me.

I was already running down the hallway though, and I took the stairs two steps at a time. Papa was still lying in bed. I heard him groan. Panting, I ran to the bed and pressed the brush against his fingers. Instinctively his hand closed around it.

"Thank heaven," I murmured.

"What are you doing?" Mama asked. She had followed me more slowly.

"Papa . . ." I panted and pointed at the brush. "I think I caught . . . his wandering soul."

Mama's face softened. She brushed the snow from my cheeks. "Sometimes we can want something so badly, it can almost feel real."

"But I felt his dream soul," I insisted.

"If you say you did." She began cleaning my hair. "Look at you. You'll catch your death of cold, and then what will I do?"

"I did what those people did in Papa's story." The laundry's warmth had yet to penetrate, and I was still shivering.

Mama made a noise in her throat as she got a spare blanket and wrapped me in it. "That's only a story," she said.

But as I looked at Papa clenching his brush, I wondered about that.

nineteen

The next morning I woke up feeling rested and refreshed after the first good sleep since Papa had taken to his bed. When I opened an eye, I saw Emily sitting up in bed and watching me. "Good morning," I said, and I meant it for the first time in a long time.

"Good morning, Joan," Emily said carefully.

Normally it took Emily a while to wake up, but she seemed fully alert.

"How long have you been up?"

"A little bit," she said.

In the past when she had woken up before me, she had climbed right over me without worrying if she would rouse me. "I think it's going to be a glorious day," I said, stretching my arms over my head so that the joints cracked.

Emily looked dubiously out the window at the gray sky, but she said, "Yes, Joan."

A quiet, polite little sister was strange enough, but it was even odder when she helped me get dressed rather than the other way around. And when I went downstairs, Bobby drew the chair away from the table so I could sit down. "I've already made breakfast."

"I'm not made of glass," I objected.

Bobby and Emily exchanged glances and then both smiled nervously. "Of course not."

"I suppose you're wondering about last night?" I asked them.

They swapped looks again. "A little," Emily said.

As they served breakfast, I tried to explain. However, the more I talked, the sillier it sounded even to me. And yet I had been sure Papa's lost soul had been with me in the study. As I saw the doubt still in their faces, I began to wonder myself. Had I been part of something magical, or was I just fooling myself?

Bobby was the first to finish, as always, but then he got up and started to wash the dishes without being asked. I normally had to shout at him to get him to do any of his chores. I thought there were some benefits to being thought crazy.

When Mama came down, I was glad to see Papa's bowl of rice gruel was empty. "How did Papa sleep?" I asked.

"Very well," Mama said with a tired smile. I suspected she had stayed up most of the night keeping watch.

I couldn't really expect Bobby and Emily to understand, because they were still young. Mama was always the levelheaded one in the family. She would tell me if last night was magic or illusion. "Mama, about last night—"

"Yes, yes," Mama said abruptly, wanting to change the subject. "Did you start up the fires in the drying room, Bobby?"

"I did," Bobby said.

However, I wasn't about to let her get off the hook that easily. "Mama, I feel like something happened."

"Really?" Mama brusquely poured a cup of cold tea for herself. "How interesting. Would you mind folding up the sheets in the back?"

"Where no one from the town can see me," I said ruefully. I thought I had my answer about last night.

Mama peered at me over the rim of her cup. "The work isn't getting done while you talk."

Still I hesitated. "Why are you ashamed of me? I did something Chinese."

Normally she would have given me a little shove in the direction she wanted me to take, but I noticed that she was keeping her distance. "I'm not ashamed of you," Mama said. "You were just upset. But I don't think you should do it again."

Suddenly I realized Mama was feeling uneasy—as if she didn't want to believe I had been brushed by real magic.

Bernice took a more down-to-earth approach when she came by that afternoon with her schoolbooks. *"I thought I would see if you wanted to do your homework like we discussed."*

I was in an old dress, the sleeves rolled up exposing my wet forearms. *"We're pretty busy since my father's been sick."*

"I hope he is recovering," Bernice said.

"He's getting there. Thank you," I said. *"Maybe we can set up a study date."*

"Go on," Mama said. "We can manage for a few hours without you. Your father would want you to put your schoolwork first."

As we went into the kitchen to work, Bernice peered curiously through the doorway at the great washtubs where the steam rose like columns to the damp ceiling. *"This is like being in the tropics."*

A red-faced Bobby staggered by with a load of laundry.

I was sure my face was still ruddy from the steam too. *"Have you visited there too?"* When she had been part of a theatrical act with her family, they had traveled all over.

"Yes," Bernice said and paused uncomfortably.

I cleared my throat. *"About last night . . ."*

Bernice glanced sideways at me. *"I assumed you were upset because of your father's illness."*

"I think there may be more to it than that." And I tried to explain briefly to her about what I had been trying to do. *"Thank you for helping me call his soul back."*

"You were upset, Joan. We could all see that."

"But you helped me," I pointed out.

Bernice patted my arm reassuringly. *"We could see it was important to you; and since you're our friend, it's important to us."* She flipped her math book open. *"Shall we begin on problem one? I just looked over our assignment briefly, and I think that's the trickiest."*

I suppose Bernice had seen too many fake magicians to believe in real magic. But perhaps she was right. As I bent to look at the page, though, I couldn't help mumbling,

"The next time Henrietta teases me, maybe I'll gnash my teeth and roll my eyes at her."

Bernice smiled. *"It might be amusing to see what would happen."*

I was glad Bernice was my friend. And I felt even happier to know I could be Chinese with her and the others. It felt good to be getting back into my normal routine, and together we started to work on our homework.

I suppose if I had taken a vote among my family and friends, they would have said it was the change in diet rather than the soul summoning that had helped Papa get better.

But I couldn't dismiss the question as easily as the others. I was still puzzling over it when I went to Miss Lucy's to borrow a book to read to Papa. While I could read some Chinese, many of his books were in classical Chinese, which was almost a completely different language from the one we spoke. Ironically, it was easier to translate an American book for him—provided the story was simple enough.

"Here." Miss Lucy selected a book. *"This is all about knights."*

I ran my finger along the spines of the books that were arranged along the shelf like soldiers. *"Miss Lucy, why do you think my father got better? Do you think it was just the change in diet and the right medicine?"*

Miss Lucy weighed the book in her hand. *"I think that had a lot to do with it, but my grandfather would have been the first to say there's a lot more to healing than just medicine."*

I made a snatching motion with my hand. *"Papa said*

that the Chinese believe we have two souls. When one of them gets lost, a person gets sick."

Miss Lucy nodded her head in sudden comprehension. *"So you were trying to call it back."*

I lowered my hand. *"I really caught it. Or at least I thought I had. It just seemed so real at the time. Do you think you can want something so much that you can make it real? Or am I just being superstitious?"*

"Stranger things have happened." Miss Lucy handed the book to me. *"There is more to the world than we know. So I've learned how to suspend disbelief. My cousin once saw an Indian fakir lie on a bed of nails without any pain and then climb a rope and disappear. He couldn't explain where the fakir went. And in my time I have seen even stranger things: I once saw a theater manager refund a customer's ticket. And when it comes to paradox, nothing can surpass the railroad schedule for strangeness."*

Miss Lucy was one person whose good opinion I wanted to keep. *"But I made a public spectacle of myself,"* I said.

Miss Lucy smiled. *"What do you care? Your father's getting stronger every day. Isn't that all you care about?"*

Miss Lucy had a way of putting her finger on the heart of things. *"I'd do it again if that's what it took,"* I admitted. And suddenly I felt as if she had lifted a burden from my shoulders.

Diet or magic, Papa was growing better and stronger every day. And that was enough. Even Emily had dropped the idea of Christmas, saying that all she wanted was a new stomach for Papa.

As I walked back to the laundry in a peaceful frame of mind, I thought it was a shame that I had to translate English stories to him. I should have been able to read Papa's beloved classics to him. Even though the idea of learning classical Chinese was daunting, I thought I should at least try.

When I went back to the laundry, I found Papa was sitting up in bed sipping tea. "What did you bring me?" A broad smile creased his face when he saw the cover. "Oh, good. I like stories about funny tin men."

I sat down in a chair. "Papa, I was thinking. Would you mind beginning the lessons again? I would like to learn more Chinese, so I can read more of your books. It's frustrating to get to the good parts and not know the key words."

Papa set his cup down on the nightstand. "I've been thinking too. Master Kung may be a bit too dry for the young ones. And literary Chinese is hard even for scholars. But you seemed to like the story about the star's tears. I'll send for some collections with stories in regular Chinese."

I felt relieved—as if I had been pardoned from ten years of hard labor. "I think we'd all like that." I found myself quickly warming to the idea. "And we'd learn something about China and the culture too."

"Your father isn't always boring." Papa picked up the brush, which he kept on the nightstand. "I thought I heard you calling me the other night."

"I was," I said.

He fussed with the tip for a moment. "I didn't think you'd been paying attention."

I opened the book on my lap. "I always listen. You just misinterpreted." Just as I had misinterpreted his quizzes about school. But I didn't know how to tell him that I had gone through his private papers.

I think he guessed from my guilty look though. "You know, Joan, we don't always tell you what a good daughter you are."

My throat caught. "It's all right, Papa."

He raised an eyebrow. "I can see what parents do here. But back home they do things differently. My parents never praised me, but I knew they loved me because they both made so many sacrifices so I could go to school."

"Just like you work long hours here," I said.

Papa seemed embarrassed by admitting that much. "Here the children think their parents have to play with them to show their love. Back home, though, parents show their love by working hard. Sometimes they kill themselves with work."

I thought of the long, hard hours they both spent in the laundry and realized how little we appreciated it—at least not until we had to do it ourselves. And I felt so bad that I took Papa's arm. "I wish you'd tell us these things," I complained.

"We shouldn't have to." Papa sighed. He played with the shaft of his brush uncomfortably. "Your mother and I do love you, even if we don't tell you every day."

After Mr. Barrington I would take Papa's good, quiet, steady brand of love any day. "I love you too, Papa."

"You're all good children. I know it can't be easy." He swung the brush from side to side. "We expect things of you, and the Americans expect things of you too. And sometimes they don't go together very well."

"It isn't always easy for any of us," I said.

"Just keep in mind the Americans are usually wrong," Papa warned.

I hid a smile. He was sounding more and more like his old self. "Yes, Papa."

That evening Papa came down to dinner with the family. We made a good, solid Chinese meal out of steamed chicken and salted vegetables over rice, and there was tea. When we were done and the table was cleared, Papa said, "I think we need Chinese games as well as Chinese lessons. How about a game of chess, Joan?"

He meant Chinese chess. When I was younger, I used to play it all the time with him, and then I had found out about American chess, which seemed so different. For one thing, there wasn't a river down the middle, and some of the rules also differed. However, what I fell in love with were the pieces, because they had shapes instead of being disks with Chinese characters. It made our chessboard (really only a sheet of paper) and the disks seem cheap in comparison. Somehow I couldn't bring myself to play Chinese chess after that, and I stopped. I couldn't remember the last time we had played.

Emily, though, slid over and sat on Papa's lap. We were all on our best behavior. "Teach Bobby and me, Papa."

Mama looked down at Emily from the kitchen sink. "Do you know the rules?"

"No, but it's time we learned," Bobby said, leaning against Papa's side.

I got the worn, familiar box down from the shelf and put it on the table. Lifting the lid, Papa spread out the paper chessboard and began to explain the symbols on the disks to Emily and Bobby.

I had barely begun to clean the dinner dishes when Papa objected, "You can't move there, Emily." And he tried to move a disk back.

"Of course, I can," Emily said simply, and moved her disk forward again. Her good behavior went only so far, apparently.

"No, you can't." Papa tried to shove it back, but Emily had kept her finger on the disk to prevent just such a possibility.

"It's my elephant," Emily stated firmly. "And I'll move it however I like."

Since Papa had also kept his finger on the disk, it looked more like some exotic form of finger wrestling than chess. "Let me explain the rules again."

As Papa went through them one more time, Emily gazed straight ahead, as if she were listening to some sound far away. She had only volunteered to play chess. She had said nothing about losing.

"Papa's just wasting his breath," I said.

Mama slipped a dish towel from a nail. "That's what I tried to tell him when you were Emily's age."

Papa glanced up and smiled. It really took very little to make him happy. He wasn't like Mr. Barrington, who needed a fancy automobile and expensive clothes. "I should have remembered. You really were the same way."

Bobby's heel kicked a leg of his chair. "What about me, Papa?"

"I could never get you to sit still long enough to listen to all the rules." Papa relinquished the disk and gave in to the inevitable. Lifting her head in triumph, Emily moved the piece where she wanted.

"I'll play the winner," I said, scraping at a pot.

Papa moved his own piece in response and raised an eyebrow at Emily. When she shook her head, he restored the piece and moved another. "It won't take long."

Like a cat loose in a tree of canaries, Emily pounced. Placing her finger upon her elephant, she made it zigzag all over the board until she could cry, "Got your general!" That was the equivalent of a king in American chess.

Papa sat back with a sigh and began to roll up his sleeves. "Your turn, Joan." Getting up, he came over to me and nudged me away from the sink. As he did so, he gave my arm a quick squeeze. It was his quiet way of thanking me.

When I took his place at the table, I said to Emily, "Supposing you explain the rules to me."

Emily was already setting out the chess pieces. "You'll learn them as we play."

"Or as you make them up," Bobby said, laughing.

Mama and Papa started to laugh too, and I couldn't help chuckling. Even Emily grinned, but she was not about to let me off the hook. My little sister checkmated me in three moves after her elephant had woven its way once again across the board like a snake through an obstacle course.

As we sat in the kitchen, I felt the warmth close round me. It felt so real, I thought I could wrap it around myself like a blanket. This feeling was why I had given in to Papa and Mama for all those years on Christmas.

I thought about poor Miss Lucy. It must be a terrible thing to outlive all of your family. I found myself wondering if she was sitting alone in her kitchen, unable to feel the same warmth though her own stove might be blazing.

As I gazed around the room at the family, I saw Papa was also drinking in the scene as he handed Mama the last plate. We smiled at one another, acknowledging the warmth we both were feeling.

Slowly he unrolled his sleeves back down to his wrists. Then he gave an abrupt nod of his head, as if he had just come to some decision. "Mama, I've been thinking over something Joan said."

"Joan is always talking," Mama said evenly. Her dish towel made squeaking sounds on the plate.

Papa took a deep breath as if he were about to plunge off a cliff. "Well, it's not good to confuse the little ones. All their friends celebrate Christmas. Why don't we let them this year?"

I could hardly believe my ears, but Mama did not miss a beat while she stacked the plate away. "We have a lot to celebrate."

Papa buttoned his cuffs. "I didn't particularly like American clothes, but even in China I put them on. I wanted to show I was modern. So why not try Christmas on for size too?"

"Thank you, Papa!" Emily said, and Bobby and I were quick to echo her.

Papa hesitated, and he reminded me of the time we had coaxed him out onto a frozen pond to skate. There had been the same look of uncertainty as he tried something new.

"And," he finally said, "thank you."

twenty 

That night Emily brought up the subject of presents again. I rolled over in our bed, turning my back to her in my impatience. "You really like to live dangerously, don't you? We're lucky to be even celebrating Christmas with Miss Lucy."

She spooned herself against my back. "I'm not talking about getting presents. I'm talking about giving them. Mama and Papa can't argue with that, can they?"

I thought that over for a moment. "I guess they can't get mad if we give them gifts."

Emily slid her arm around my waist. "This will be the best Christmas of all," she said.

"It should be. It's our first Christmas," I said, but she was already asleep.

There weren't a lot of days to get ready for Christmas, but no one complained. I knew Emily was making kites for everyone because she had just learned how to do that in school. And suddenly string began disappearing from the laundry ball that we used to wrap the parcels of clean clothes.

I didn't know what Bobby was making, but he was always over at Miss Lucy's. That made for problems when Emily worked on her presents over there too. Miss Lucy solved the dilemma by assigning Bobby to the kitchen and Emily to the parlor.

I wasn't sure what to do about presents, but then I remembered the embroidery lessons Mama had once tried to give me. I had only been about Emily's age and hadn't been much interested in it, so Mama and I had stopped by mutual agreement. I used some of my allowance to buy several fine Irish linen handkerchiefs from a millinery store, and I began to embroider ornate monograms on them, copying the elaborate Gothic letters in one of Miss Lucy's books. Mama's and Papa's I did in the Chinese characters of their names. (I worked in the guest bedroom at Miss Lucy's.)

And when Christmas Eve finally rolled around, we even enjoyed church, because they used real animals for the pageant, and the donkey had an accident right in the middle of the cardboard stable.

Emily was still giggling about it when we crossed the street with Miss Lucy. Miss Lucy was swinging Emily's hand back and forth as if they were both small girls. *"Well,"* she confessed, *"this is the most fragrant Christmas I can remember. Next year I hope they go back to people in animal costumes."*

The laundry was dark as we threaded our way down the alley to Miss Lucy's.

"I be right back," Mama said, disappearing inside our kitchen for a moment.

As we stood outside Miss Lucy's, I realized that too many of my friends took Christmas for granted. What had they gone through to value it as we did?

"Now we start," Mama said, coming back out with a bag.

Willy came out of Miss Lucy's house at that moment. He was a thin, loose-limbed man with a shapeless felt hat on his head. In his arms he had a ladder. He was a general handyman who did odd jobs for everyone, including Miss Lucy.

"It's all done, Miss Lucy," he said.

Miss Lucy let go of Emily's hand and snapped open her purse. *"Thank you, Willy. You and your wife stop by tomorrow for your present."*

As she handed him a dollar, Willy tipped his hat. *"If I can ever get Mabel out of the kitchen. Once she gets to baking Christmas gifts, it's hard to make her stop."*

"Well, see that you do." Miss Lucy laughed. Shutting her purse, she took Emily's hand again. *"This is my next-favorite part of Christmas,"* she said to us. She was as excited as Emily, so she didn't even wait to put on the lights, but instead started to tug off her galoshes. The rest of us copied her, but in our eagerness—even Mama and Papa—we tumbled them together into a pile. We would have a time sorting them out later.

It is always an odd moment when you first free your shoes from galoshes. You lose that sensation of sweaty heat. As I stood there in the darkness, I noticed the smell of fruit.

"Oranges," Bobby sniffed and murmured in wonder. They filled the cold kitchen with their fragrance.

Miss Lucy lit a gas jet to reveal a whole bowl of fruit and nuts on the table. *"All the way from Florida,"* Miss Lucy said. *"And there are nuts from Brazil and all sorts of places. Enough nuts even for Bobby."*

The fragrance from the fruit filled the room like an expensive perfume. At some other time of the year I would have taken the fruit and nuts for granted, but in winter it seemed wonderfully, gloriously extravagant. I just hoped that Miss Lucy hadn't gone overboard with the expenses.

I rolled an orange around in my palms, savoring the texture, the roundness, the scent. For a moment I felt almost as grand as Victoria. I wondered what her unspoken wish might have been during our last meeting. Was it to stay longer? Was it to be my friend? It still made me feel sad and angry inside to think of her.

"Joan, come on." Emily was fairly dancing with impatience as she stood with Miss Lucy in the hallway door.

Putting the orange back into the bowl, I caught her other hand, and we let Miss Lucy lead us. At the threshold of the parlor, Miss Lucy let go of Emily's hand.

Emily's mouth fell open. *"Oh,"* she said breathlessly, and then she took a small step and then another, as if she were afraid to break the illusion. *"Oh, oh, oh."* With each exclamation she tiptoed farther into the room.

As he followed her, Bobby whispered, *"Wow."*

Miss Lucy stood beside the doorway. *"Please come in, Joan."*

It was strange, but I felt as if my feet had been glued

to the hallway just in front of the door.

Mama gave me a good-natured nudge. "Go on. What are you waiting for? This is what you've nagged us for all these years."

And I realized that was the reason I was afraid to go in. After waiting for fifteen years for this moment, I was wondering if anything could match the anticipation and my imagination.

I think Miss Lucy understood a little of what was going through my mind, because she took my wrist. Little points of light danced over her eyeglass lenses, so her eyes seemed lost behind a cloud of stars. *"Please."*

I felt light as a kite as Miss Lucy drew me into her parlor. All of her family's odd paraphernalia had been shoved into one corner so Willy could set up her tree.

Emily and Bobby were standing in front of it in awe. It soared ten feet to the ceiling and filled the room with the smell of pine. Lighted candles perched on each branch like fiery little birds. We had helped Miss Lucy string popcorn and cranberries beforehand, and in the candlelight the strings hung like ropes of pearls and rubies hanging in the green shadowy boughs.

My voice caught for a moment as I gazed at the tree ablaze in all its glory. *"It's beautiful."*

So beautiful, it hurt.

"Merry Christmas," Miss Lucy said with a clap of her hands.

I held my breath, sure that the tree would vanish with that loud clap, but it stayed. Still, Bobby, Emily and I were afraid to speak.

It was Mama and Papa who reminded us of our

manners. *"Merry Christmas,"* they said to Miss Lucy.

We turned belatedly then and wished her the same.

If anything, Miss Lucy was even more excited as she practically skipped toward the tree. *"Now what are these packages here? Help me read them, Emily."* There was a pile of packages wrapped in red tissue paper.

The anticipation built inside me until I felt like a bottle of soda pop that had been shaken up. And all that fizziness was whirling around and piling up ready to explode. Bobby too was more restless and jiggly than ever. Even Mama and Papa couldn't hide their excitement as they sat, waiting.

Emily's hands shook as she looked at each tag and announced the name in a voice shrill with anticipation.

When all the packages had been distributed, I glanced at Mama and Papa. However, they didn't seem upset. I guess they wanted to celebrate the fact that Papa was alive. And perhaps I'd been right: Who can get mad at someone who gives you a present?

Bobby insisted that the first gifts we opened up should be the ones he had given us. Each of us wound up getting our very own decorated walnut shell. Emily handled hers unenthusiastically. "I bet it was more fun eating the walnuts."

I nudged her. "It's the thought that counts."

"That's my point exactly," Emily said, but she forced herself to kiss Bobby—an act of gratitude that neither enjoyed much.

Everyone politely admired the embroidered handkerchiefs I had given them—even Mama, though she scrutinized the stitchery on hers by holding it near a candle on the tree. Of course, Bobby tried out his right then and there.

And my parents and Miss Lucy both said they hoped spring would come soon so they could try out Emily's kites.

"Yes, I can't wait," I said, and dug my elbow into Bobby's side.

"Yeah, me too," he said.

Papa shook his package, which was about the size of his thumb. *"This too small for kite."* For Miss Lucy's sake he was speaking English.

Emily knelt next to him. *"I thought all that running around with a kite might upset your stomach too much."*

"*What is it?*" Papa tore away the paper excitedly and then held up a bookmark. *"How pretty."*

Emily traced its outline with her fingertip. *"It's like a tear from a star."* I remembered Papa's story about the star that had wept.

That pleased Papa more than the present. His hand closed around it. *"So you remember."*

Miss Lucy leaned in curiously. *"It sounds like there's a story behind it."*

"It's a very lovely Chinese story," Emily said. *"Papa will tell it to you sometime."*

Papa glanced at Miss Lucy shyly. *"You not want hear old stuff. You just think superst-stitious,"* Papa stuttered the unfamiliar word.

"Oh, but I would," Miss Lucy said.

Unused to all the attention, Papa was feeling both proud and embarrassed at the same time. *"No, Joan do better job. She tell."*

And so I promised Miss Lucy that I would tell her about the orphan and the star that had wept diamond tears.

"Don't forget these," Miss Lucy said. Reaching behind the Christmas tree, she brought out packages for both Mama and Papa.

Mama eyed the present in distress. *"You say adults not exchange gifts,"* Mama protested.

"Having an excuse to celebrate Christmas is a nice enough present for me." Miss Lucy was so pleased with herself that she was bouncing up and down on the balls of her feet.

When Mama took her gift, she cradled it in her arms uncertainly. Despite his best efforts, Papa could not resist tearing at a corner of his. *"Not hug,"* he admonished her. *"Like this."*

"I know," Mama said, and tore at the other corner. Together they ripped through the wrapping as fast as Bobby would have. I could see where he got his ripping technique from.

Mama and Papa both got mufflers and mittens from Miss Lucy.

Mama admired her bright-red muffler. We'd never lose her in a snowstorm if she wore that. *"You knit yourself?"* she ask Miss Lucy.

Miss Lucy imitated knitting furiously with invisible needles. *"It keeps the circulation going in my hands."*

Papa wound his purple muffler around his neck. *"It handsome, very handsome."*

"I used purple just like the emperors of ancient Rome," Miss Lucy explained. *"I hope you don't mind."*

"Yes?" Papa stroked the muffler end that dangled down his chest. *"In China, emperor wear yellow."*

"Is that a fact?" Miss Lucy said, fascinated. *"I'd love to learn more. In fact, the women's group at the church would too. Would you consider lecturing to us sometime on China?"*

Papa's ears actually turned almost the same shade of red as Mama's muffler. *"I not talk English good."*

Miss Lucy was trying her best to forge a bridge between them. *"And I can't speak Chinese at all. You certainly speak well enough to communicate your ideas. So please, think about it."*

Mama was almost preening. "You're a teacher. Teach," she coaxed Papa in Chinese.

Papa gave a little shrug, but he promised Miss Lucy, *"I think about."*

"Please do," Miss Lucy said to him, and then asked Bobby to get the large package from behind the tree.

When he brought it out, he read the tag. *"It's for me."* The next instant he disappeared in a cloud of torn paper. *"A sled!"* he said. As the fragments settled, we could see him hugging the wooden top against his chest.

Miss Lucy caressed the side of one runner. *"It was my old one. I had Willy sharpen the runners and repaint the wood so it's good as new."*

Papa took it from Bobby and held it up to admire how the candlelight gleamed off the red sides and along the edges of the runners. *"Pretty."*

Miss Lucy grinned and winked at me. *"I used to go lickety-split down the boys' hill."*

I leaned my head back, startled. *"Miss Lucy, you're wicked."*

"I was a caution," she said, wagging a finger at me. *"So learn from my mistakes."*

Emily had slipped around behind the tree to find her present. She tore the paper off nearly as fast as Bobby. Give her a couple of years and she would probably be just as devastating.

"Oh," she said in ecstasy. She cradled the doll in her arms, rocking gently back and forth. The doll's curls gleamed like gold in the candlelight, and when Emily dipped the head downward experimentally, the ice-blue eyes shut; when she raised the head, the eyes snapped open. She massaged the doll's hair and pink cheeks as if she could not believe it was real. *"It's lovely."*

"Whenever we went for a walk on Main Street, I saw how you looked at it," Miss Lucy said lovingly. Then she got a small gift from behind the tree and presented it to me.

"Thank you," I said, putting it on my lap.

I started to rip it open like Emily and Bobby, but Miss Lucy warned me, *"Careful."*

So I took my time. When I had removed the wrapping, I stared at the object on my lap. Resting there was the fairy light. It caught the light of the tree candles, burning like a miniature sunset.

Trembling, I held it up in my palms to catch the light better. *"But I thought you sold this with all your other things."*

"Not that. I saw how much you liked it," Miss Lucy said. *"I used to sneak into my parents' bedroom and peek*

at it just the same way. It used to be on my mother's dresser. Finally one Christmas she gave it to me and said, 'Some things you don't really own. You're just taking care of them for a while before you pass them on to the next generation.'"

"You have other things from her?" Mama asked.

"No, this is all that's left," Miss Lucy admitted.

"Then Joan can't keep," Mama said, and directed me to give it back.

Miss Lucy refused, though. *"I don't have children of my own. At least on this little matter, please let me share yours."*

Papa put a hand on Mama's arm and said to Miss Lucy, *"Yes, of course."* And that perhaps was his special gift to Miss Lucy this Christmas.

It only made me feel guilty. I thought of how I had helped the Barringtons cheat her. *"I don't deserve it,"* I said.

"Of course you do, dear." She leaned forward to kiss my cheek; but before she did, she whispered in my ear. *"It's Christmas. Forgive them as I have. When you do that, you'll be able to forgive yourself."*

And suddenly I felt all my anger wash away. Wherever Victoria was, I wished her a happy Christmas. And in the spirit of the season, I even hoped that for Mr. Barrington.

"I'll treasure it always," I promised.

"Now open ours. This is for all you." Mama reached beneath her chair and took out the bag she had gotten from the laundry. From it, she lifted a cylinder wrapped in an old advertising flier. *"But be careful."*

Bobby cradled it in both hands. *"It's heavy."*

Emily started to reach for it in frustration. "*Open it.*"

"*Careful,*" Mama warned. "*Joan, you do.*"

Bobby surrendered it reluctantly. Hastily I ripped away the paper to reveal a glass jar with Chinese words on it. "*What is it?*" Emily demanded.

"*It preserved fruit.*" From the bag Mama produced three pairs of chopsticks that she had also stowed there. "*It come from China. We have cousin send us all way from San Francisco. It is . . .*" She corrected her mistake with a little frown. "*Was for Chinese New Year, but tonight special too.*"

On her instructions Bobby opened it, and then Mama dipped a chopstick into the reddish-purple paste. "*You stir chopstick around. Then you lift out. Then you lick.*" She held it out toward Emily, who leaned her head in and licked it tentatively at first.

"*Mm,*" she said, and, taking the chopstick from Mama, began to lick at it enthusiastically. "*I can taste the sunshine.*"

Mama sat back happily—the way you do when an experiment succeeds. "*Now you, Bobby,*" she said, handing him a chopstick.

As Emily licked her paste, she kept an eagle eye on Bobby as he swirled his chopstick around and started to lift it out. "*Hey, you're taking too much.*"

Papa patted Emily's shoulder to calm her down. "*There plenty.*"

Mama looked as if there were many memories she wanted to share, but her English wasn't up to it. I made a note to myself to ask her later in Chinese.

"This my favorite at home," Mama declared and gave me a chopstick. *"You try, Joan."*

When I did, I thought Emily was right. *"It does taste like sunshine,"* I said. And I thought myself to some warm, sun-drenched orchard in China. It was amazing to think that it had come some nine thousand miles to us.

"Papa and me, we think you children should know sweets from home," Mama said, and smiled in triumph at completing a complicated thought in English. Then she politely held out a clean chopstick to Miss Lucy. *"Now you, Miss Lucy."*

Miss Lucy put up her hands self-consciously. *"Oh, no, something this special should only be for your family."*

"You family," Mama said, and thrust the chopstick into Miss Lucy's hand.

"How can I refuse an invitation when it's worded like that?" Miss Lucy sampled it then, giving little smacks of her lips. *"You can really taste the fruit."*

However, when it was Mama's turn, she barely scraped the preserves.

"Take more, Mama," I urged.

"I just want enough to remember," Mama said, licking her chopstick.

Papa took even less than Mama, and I thought it was typical of their sacrifices. That was how they really expressed their love—not with a lot of lies like Mr. Barrington.

"It poetry of fruit," he said, satisfied. And even rarer in America than Miss Lucy's oranges and nuts.

While waiting for her next turn to sample the jar,

Emily had drifted over to the window. *"It's snowing outside,"* she crowed.

It looked as if a giant feather pillow had burst outside. The window framed the street, where the snow had already transformed the roofs into fluffy white wigs and the gables into bushy eyebrows. In the whirling snowflakes, the windows themselves seemed to glow like soft golden eyes.

Perhaps it was his illness, or maybe it was the spirit of the season, but for once even Papa seemed to enjoy snow. *"When inside it warm, even snow look pretty."*

Emily whirled and clutched at his arm. *"Why don't you take the day off tomorrow, Papa?"*

Papa tried to shrug her question off. *"If laundry not open, no money."* No one worked longer or harder than Papa.

"You weren't going to work on Christmas?" Miss Lucy asked in surprise.

"Well, I . . ." He hesitated.

Mama gave him a nudge. "Oh, go on."

"It's robbing the children," Papa said stubbornly. "You said yourself they need new shoes."

Mama gave him another nudge. "You'll just be sitting around the whole day. No one's going to want their laundry on Christmas."

"There could be an emergency." Papa took pride in being a professional.

Mama laughed. "What kind of emergency could it be? We're a laundry."

"Maybe they'll be out of socks," Papa said.

This time when Mama tried to nudge Papa, he slipped

to the side and she missed. "Then the sockless will find you," she said, straightening back up.

Papa stared down at Emily's upturned, hopeful face. It was hard for Papa to break one of his own rules. "*Maybe half day,*" he finally said.

Emily immediately began to plan out his schedule. "*First, we'll work on a snowwoman.*"

Bobby picked up his sled. "*We can try it out tomorrow,*" he said excitedly.

"*Why wait?*" Papa asked exuberantly.

I watched in amazement as Papa enthusiastically began to bundle himself back into his clothes. In his haste, though, he let his muffler hang down loosely and did not even button up his coat.

We had to go back into the kitchen and sort through the galoshes. Amazingly, Papa was the first out the door, ahead of even Bobby.

"*Wait for me,*" Emily complained.

"*Emily's the old maid,*" Miss Lucy teased as she headed outside.

"*I am not.*" In frustration, Emily stamped her feet into the galoshes.

By the time Mama and I finished dressing, Papa and Miss Lucy had gone through the alley and had reached Main. There they were busily towing Emily on the sled along the snow-filled street as she urged them into pursuit of the laughing Bobby. Every now and then he paused long enough to fling handfuls of fresh snow at them.

Mama hooked her arm with mine for support as we followed along their tracks. The runners of the sled had carved curving designs in the street, but the snowfall was already softening and filling them up.

Snowflakes hung on Mama's hair and eyelashes, so they seemed to be changing into threads of snow. "Mama, you're turning into a snowwoman."

She brushed my hair and cheeks. "So are you."

As Papa and Miss Lucy played with Bobby and Emily, the space increased between them and us. At a distance under the streetlight they seemed like merry shadows, whirling and dancing across a white canvas, too alive to stay fixed in one place.

Mama paused and then shook her head. "You know, I think the sled may be the first toy Papa ever played with."

I stopped in surprise. "He didn't have toys when he was a boy?"

"He had books," she said. "It was all his family could afford."

Ahead of us Papa had made the tactical mistake of opening his mouth to laugh. Instantly, he had caught a mouthful of snow—which made it all the harder for him to laugh as he spluttered. "Well," I said, "he seems to be making up for lost time."

The snowfall had suddenly increased, and Miss Lucy's and our family's shadows dissolved in a world of swirling bits of white, snowy lace. Underfoot, the ugly mud and slush had vanished beneath the new coating of snow. A fresh canvas. A new snowfall.

"You're good children," Mama said. "You won't get too spoiled if your papa has fun with you."

And the truth came to me just like a match flaring on

a dark moonless night. Until then, though I had been enjoying myself, I hadn't really been feeling the spirit of Christmas yet. All the effervescence I had felt before had stayed bottled up inside. Now as I felt happy for Papa, I also felt all those tiny bubbles release inside, and every one of those bubbles was as golden as sunlight as it exploded. I was so giddy that I thought I could have floated out of the dark winter to the land of the stars.

Before I could describe that wonderful feeling to Mama, a snowball flew out of the whiteness. *"Got you,"* Emily shouted.

As if through a beaded white curtain, I vaguely made out Emily's outline jumping up and down gleefully. With her were Bobby, Miss Lucy, and Papa, who had still kept the sled in tow.

As I wiped snow from my mouth, I decided that insight would have to wait until after revenge. *"I'll show you,"* I called.

Mama had already squatted down and was flinging handfuls of snow toward our attackers. She was laughing as merrily as a young girl as she rose, went a few more steps, and bent over to throw more snow.

"Wait for me, Mama," I said, and went to join her.

Afterword

As I said in the preface, this is a work of fiction, but such stories as the flight from the bull and the sledding have long been part of my family's lore. So have the stories about Christmas with the real Miss Lucy, Miss Alcinda Davisson. (She too used "Bull Mooser" as a disparaging remark.)

I want to thank Dwight Fowler for showing me around some of my family's later haunts in Bridgeport and for clearing up puzzles about my family's life there. In general I want to extend my gratitude to the West Virginians who made me feel so welcome during my visits.

There are many Asians who suffer from lactose intolerance. As a child I couldn't understand why so many old-timers stayed away from ice cream. It was only later—when I was older but not necessarily wiser—that I did.